PINE ISLAND
VISITORS

ALSO BY POLLY HORVATH

An Occasional Cow
(Pictures by Gioia Fiammenghi)

No More Cornflakes

The Happy Yellow Car

When the Circus Came to Town

The Trolls

Everything on a Waffle

The Canning Season

The Vacation

The Pepins and Their Problems
(Pictures by Marylin Hafner)

The Corps of the Bare-Boned Plane

My One Hundred Adventures

Northward to the Moon

Mr. and Mrs. Bunny—Detectives Extraordinaire!
(Pictures by Sophie Blackall)

One Year in Coal Harbor

Lord and Lady Bunny—Almost Royalty!
(Pictures by Sophie Blackall)

The Night Garden

Very Rich

Pine Island Home

PINE ISLAND VISITORS

Polly Horvath

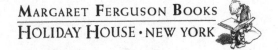

MARGARET FERGUSON BOOKS
HOLIDAY HOUSE · NEW YORK

Margaret Ferguson Books

HOLIDAY HOUSE is registered in the U.S. Patent and Trademark Office.
Printed and bound in August 2023 at Maple Press, York, PA, USA.
www.holidayhouse.com
First Edition
1 3 5 7 9 10 8 6 4 2

Library of Congress Cataloging-in-Publication Data

Names: Horvath, Polly, author.
Title: Pine Island visitors / Polly Horvath.
Description: First edition. | New York : Holiday House, [2023] | "Margaret
 Ferguson Books." | Audience: Ages 9-12. | Audience: Grades 4-6. | Summary:
 The McCready sisters have just settled into their new home on Pine Island when
 they get word that an unwelcome houseguest is coming to visit for months.
Identifiers: LCCN 2022052059 | ISBN 9780823452958 (hardcover)
Subjects: CYAC: Sisters—Fiction. | Orphans—Fiction. | Eccentrics and
 eccentricities—Fiction. | British Columbia—Fiction.
Classification: LCC PZ7.H79224 Pj 2023 | DDC [Fic]—dc23
LC record available at https://lccn.loc.gov/2022052059

ISBN: 978-0-8234-5295-8 (hardcover)

For Liam and Emily and Becca and Robbie

Contents

PINE ISLAND VISITORS

The Letter

It was September. School was about to begin. The McCready sisters, Fiona, fifteen, Marlin, thirteen, Natasha, ten, and Charlie, eight, were settled into their Pine Island home, their routines, and their new life after arriving on the island the previous March. Their parents had died the year before and Mrs. Weatherspoon, the woman from their church who had been caring for them in Borneo, had found a great-aunt on Pine Island off the west coast of Canada who had agreed to take them. But when the girls landed there they found their great-aunt had died suddenly, leaving them stranded. After a frightening few months when they didn't know what would become of them, trying to keep their adultless existence a secret so social services couldn't take over and perhaps split them up, their neighbor and their great-aunt's former suitor, Al Farber, had decided to adopt them. This brought finally a measure of calm and security to the girls' lives and for the month of August they had been able to relax a little and enjoy the summer, each in the way that suited her best.

Marlin, who had written a cookbook that Al, also a writer, was trying to help her get published, had started a second book in what she now called "my series." She was playing with a new cake recipe while Charlie sat at the kitchen counter.

"My new book is called *Thirty Cakes a Twelve-Year-Old Could Make and* Did! But I have to be honest, I have my reservations about using twelve when I am thirteen," she admitted to Charlie.

Marlin's first book was called *Thirty Meals a Twelve-Year-Old Could Make and* Did! And she was planning another book called *A Year of Holiday Dinners a Twelve-Year-Old Could Make and* Did!

Marlin was twelve when she discovered cooking and writing. And twelve when she started creating and testing her own recipes. She thought twelve sounded better than thirteen. Twelve was a child. Thirteen was a teenager and it seemed a little less laudable for a teenager to be able to make meals and cakes and holiday dinners.

"Suppose someone is interviewing me," Marlin went on, "and they ask how old I am and I say twelve like the book title and then they expose me as a fraud?"

"Can you go to jail for that?" asked Charlie.

"I doubt it," said Marlin. "But it would be bad publicity."

"When are they going to publish your first book?" asked

Charlie, who had had the publishing process explained to her by Marlin and Al both but still asked this question.

"I keep telling you, we don't know," snapped Marlin. This was a sore point with her. "No one has bought it yet, Charlie. It won't be published until someone buys it."

Marlin knew Charlie wasn't trying to poke her, that she could never quite grasp the idea that you had to keep sending a book out over and over and getting rejection slips and trying again. That it wasn't a question of just writing it and someone buying it, no matter how good a book it was. "It's being sent to some smaller publishers now. We got a no from the big ones."

"Who is we? I thought this was just your book," said Charlie, eating bits of baking chocolate that Marlin was shaving into cake batter.

"We means me and my agent, Steve," said Marlin while she batted Charlie's hand away from the chocolate. "Stop that, I'm grating this for the cake."

"I thought Steve was Al's agent," said Charlie.

"Well, he is but when that first agent dropped me Al was finally able to persuade Steve to send out my book but he hasn't had much luck either."

"What's the name of this cake?" asked Charlie.

"The red devil," said Marlin, relieved that they had changed the subject. After the sixth rejection from the smaller publishers, the whole topic made her anxious. "It's a Halloween cake. I'm going to make it into a devil's head with horns. The flavor is devil's food with extra dark chocolate shaved in."

"I liked the lemon meringue cake," said Charlie. "The one that looked like a smiling sun for the first day of summer. The first day of summer should be a bigger holiday. With balloons."

"Yeah, that one was okay," said Marlin absently, her mind back on why her Thirty Meals book had been rejected.

"Will this one have a meringue frosting?"

"No, this one is a buttercream frosting that's decorated. Red. Thus the red devil. I'm making the horns out of pate a choux dough—that's the pastry for things like cream puffs and éclairs—and I'm putting green whipped cream inside them."

"That sounds gross," said Charlie.

"It's not. It's going to be delicious," said Marlin.

"School starts tomorrow," said Charlie for the umpteenth time that day. Marlin wondered if Charlie really thought they didn't remember or if she thought she must repeat it to make it real. She wondered if Charlie was nervous about school starting but that was unlikely. Charlie had a best friend, Ashley, with whom she did everything and when Charlie had a best friend she was rarely worried about things like a new teacher or classroom.

"Yes, I know," said Marlin.

"And still no dog," said Charlie.

Fiona came in and sat next to Charlie.

"You know Al said we could get a dog or two once we decide what kind we want," Fiona reminded her.

"I want a smooth collie," said Charlie. "Ashley has a smooth collie."

"We can't get some dog just because Ashley has one," said Fiona.

"You have to make sure the breed is a good match for your family," said Natasha, joining them.

"I want a boxer," said Marlin. "The breed book Al bought us says they are silly but courageous."

"I want a beagle," said Natasha.

"I want a black German shepherd. Here, look." Fiona fetched the breed book, opened it, and showed them images. "Doesn't it look like something out of a fairy tale?"

"It looks like a wolf," said Charlie disapprovingly.

"Maybe we could *get* a wolf," said Natasha. "I changed my mind. I don't want a beagle now, I want a wolf."

"You can't have a wolf," said Fiona. "They aren't domestic animals."

"I know that," said Natasha. "But dogs weren't domestic animals once. Horses weren't domestic animals once. Cats weren't domestic animals once. It's all about adaptation and training."

"That is so not like you," said Marlin to Natasha. "You know wild animals shouldn't be kept as pets."

"I know," said Natasha. Her face was a study in conflict between what she knew was right and what she wanted. "I still want a wolf."

"A wolf would pretend to be your friend and then eat you in the middle of the night," said Charlie.

"That's nonsense," said Natasha.

"I've read 'Little Red Riding Hood,'" said Charlie.

"Some people breed dogs with wolves but I don't think it works out well," said Fiona. "It's too bad. They have that lovely cry."

The girls sometimes heard the call of the British Columbian coastal wolves, native to Pine Island. It was loud and echoey and the voices harmonized as if the wolves were the best of a cappella singers. The pitch of one howl blending seamlessly into the next.

"I guess if I can't have a wolf, beagles are my second choice," said Natasha.

"Beagles howl," said Fiona. "Have you heard them online?" She pulled up a YouTube video of howling beagles. "Can you imagine that, especially if we had two when Al was trying to work? He doesn't seem wildly enthusiastic about a dog to begin with. Can you imagine if we had noisy dogs?"

"Not all smooth collies bark a lot," said Charlie. "I've

been over to Ashley's house when her dog didn't bark once the whole time I was there. Not even when I came to the door."

"Maybe," said Natasha, "but it says right here"—she flipped the book to smooth collies—"'The breed is inclined to bark.' So maybe you will get two that don't bark, but it's unlikely."

"German shepherds bark," said Charlie.

"Where did you read *that*?" asked Fiona, noting that this whole pet discussion seemed to have come down to which dog breed would be least likely to annoy Al.

"Maybe we should just get cats," said Natasha. "They're very quiet. They could live in the house. We could get one for each of us."

"I don't like cats," said Marlin. "They're too slithery."

"I don't mind cats but I hate litter boxes. They smell," said Fiona.

"Oh, I forgot litter boxes," said Natasha. "I don't want cats then either."

"We're not getting cats anyway, we're getting *dogs*," said Charlie, who looked as if she were about to cry. She found being the youngest difficult. Too often things veered out of her control.

Just then the phone rang. Fiona answered it and passed it to Charlie. It was Ashley. When Charlie hung up she looked excited. "Ashley's dog breeder called Ashley's parents to tell them they have a female they might start breeding."

"That's great," said Fiona. "But we haven't decided on a smooth collie. We have to be in agreement."

"If we had two dogs we could call them Stick and Feather," said Charlie.

"Those are very weird names," said Marlin.

"They just came to me," said Charlie. "I woke in the middle of the night and said, Stick and Feather."

Marlin had put the cake in the oven and already the wonderful smell of baking chocolate cake wafted through the kitchen.

"Do you have your clothes laid out for school tomorrow and your backpack packed with all your school supplies?" Marlin asked Charlie.

"Not yet," said Charlie.

"Then you'd better do it now," said Marlin. "You know what you're like in the morning and it's going to be hard after a whole summer of sleeping in to have to get up for the school bus."

Charlie went upstairs to organize herself while Marlin, who made dinner for all of them every night, put the lasagna in the oven with the cake. Then she made a salad and set the table.

Natasha went back to the office that had been their aunt's and housed their aunt's big desk, walls of books, and her big computer, all of which, of course, now belonged to the girls but which they still thought of as their aunt's, and sat there looking up dog breeds. She thought there must be a dog breed that was descended from wolves and if there was she would find it somewhere on the internet.

Fiona was upstairs taking a bath and worrying about school the next day. In June she had stood up her new boyfriend, Davy Clement, in an embarrassing situation made worse by being unable to tell him why she had stood him up. She had sent Marlin to tell him she couldn't meet him but he was gone before Marlin could do so. She had not seen him in town all summer although she had ridden her bicycle about aimlessly all over St. Mary's By the Sea, the small town closest to the girls, hoping to run into him. As time went by, the idea of running into him with such a huge misunderstanding between them became more and more a hideous problem looming on the horizon and she found herself avoiding those very streets she had gone down before hoping to see him.

Whereas last spring Fiona had liked her new school, now she was dreading a return to it. She had not been able to make any close friends when she and her sisters arrived on Pine Island and started their new schools because she had needed to guard the secret of living without an adult. Now without that impediment she should be looking forward to a fresh start and finally making a couple of close friends. Instead, here she was with a giant knot in her stomach about having to face Davy. She still could not bring herself to tell him the truth, that Al had been too drunk to drive her to the dance and she had been crying too hard to bike to the school to explain. It was partially because it seemed disloyal to Al to reveal this to anyone, Al who in the end had saved them all. But mostly because it was shameful, having an adoptive guardian who had gotten too drunk to drive even though he had since given up drinking.

Mercifully Marlin put an end to these thoughts by calling, "Dinner!" and Fiona got dressed and went downstairs.

The girls were gathering at the table when Al came in.

"Well!" he said, breezily, sitting down. "Summer's over. School tomorrow!"

"Yes," said Fiona, putting down the salad and setting an extra place for Al while Marlin dished out the lasagna by the stove. He didn't often eat with them and they never knew when to expect it. Usually they brought his supper to the trailer he lived in behind the house or he came in to grab some to go.

"Strings for you, Natasha!" said Al.

"Yes," said Natasha, smiling down into her plate.

Natasha had wanted to rent a violin, take violin lessons, and join the strings group at school but before Al had adopted them the girls hadn't been able to afford it.

"I'm showing my new pencil case to Ashley tomorrow," said Charlie. "Hers is a penguin. She said she never saw a shark one. I may have the only shark one at school!"

"Since you got it at Walmart that is very unlikely," said Marlin.

Al had taken the girls to Shoreline, the larger city an hour away where any serious shopping was done. St. Mary's By the Sea had only a few stores on its tiny main street.

"I like school but it takes a lot of time away from my writing and baking experiments," said Marlin importantly.

"If that's how you feel, you're not a real writer yet," said Al. "Real writers will do anything to avoid writing. A real writer would positively welcome a chance to go to school to escape writing for a while."

"That doesn't make sense," said Charlie.

"It does if you're a writer," said Al, digging into his food without waiting for everyone to be served.

Charlie started to do the same but Fiona eyed her sternly as the salad was being passed around. The girls had been brought up with strict table manners and Fiona felt she had to hold fast to them in the face of Al's more laissez-faire ways.

"Anyhow, Marlin," Al went on, "think of school as a pleasant distraction. I wish I had some way to avoid the blank page."

"You could go dog-shopping," said Charlie.

"That's your job," said Al jovially. "Perhaps I should

buy a cell phone and waste time as your age group does, Fiona, constantly staring at it."

This was a sore point. The phone Mrs. Weatherspoon had bought the girls in Borneo had run out of minutes. Before Fiona could buy more, Natasha had taken the phone with her up to the oceanside cliffs, hoping to photograph some birds without realizing the phone had no camera, and had dropped it into the ocean. The girls had Aunt Martha's landline but Fiona still thought they needed a cell. But she wanted a real one with a real phone plan and data. When Fiona told Al all this, instead of being sympathetic, he lectured the girls about the idiocy of cell phones. Marlin had called him a Luddite and Al had been so impressed that she knew the word Luddite, he hadn't even minded being called one but after that Al was constantly lecturing the girls about the evils of cell phones and Fiona was heartily sick of it.

He was unusually merry that evening and Fiona couldn't help thinking it was because the next day they would all be back in school and no one would be knocking on his trailer door interrupting his work every half hour as she feared the younger girls had done all too often that summer.

"Everything's so much better going to school this time," said Charlie. "I have a friend. I don't have to keep some stupid secret. We're going to get a *dog*."

"And I've got strings," said Natasha.

"And, Fiona, I guess you're going to have to make nice with that boy again, what was his name?" said Al. He heaped salad on his plate and when she didn't reply, reminded her. "The one you stood up."

Fiona blushed beet red. She couldn't believe Al had brought this up. Especially since it had been *his* fault. She looked at her napkin. While she tried to frame a response, Marlin looked at Fiona and changed the subject. "Hey, did anyone get the mail today?"

"It's Labor Day," said Natasha. "There is no mail."

"Oh, jeez, speaking of mail, I've been carrying this around since Friday. I forgot all about it," said Al. He stood up and reached into his back jeans pocket and pulled out a crumpled pink envelope and threw it across the table at Marlin.

"Whew! It reeks of roses," said Marlin. "Someone must have sprayed a whole bottle of perfume on it."

"Who writes to us?" asked Natasha.

"On scented stationery," said Fiona, glad for a change in subject.

"I hope it isn't time-sensitive," said Marlin. "You've had it since *Friday*?"

"I shoved it into my back pocket on the way to town. I guess I forgot it because you girls never get mail."

"I'd think that would make you remember it *more*," said Marlin.

"Who's it addressed to?" asked Fiona.

"'The McCready sisters,'" read Marlin. "Curiouser and curiouser."

"Curiouser isn't a word," said Natasha.

"It's a quote from *Alice in Wonderland*, ignoramus," said Marlin. "And actually, it *is* a word." She ripped the envelope open and read the pink sheets inside front and back swiftly, her frown deepening until she finally groaned, "Oh, no. No! No! No!"

"What? Who's it from?" Fiona leaned over and grabbed it from her. She looked at the signature at the bottom of the page. "Mrs. Weatherspoon! Why didn't she just email?"

Fiona read Mrs. Weatherspoon's spidery handwriting as quickly as she could; then she too looked upset.

"Oh, *JEEZ!*" said Fiona. The other girls looked at her in alarm. Fiona always tried to keep things positive.

"I *like* Mrs. Weatherspoon," said Charlie, who couldn't understand why her sisters were looking so upset.

"I like her too, Charlie," began Fiona.

"But not for…I mean I thought we were done with her," Marlin whispered. "I know that sounds creepy but…"

"What do you mean?" asked Natasha.

"She says she's coming to visit. To be our houseguest. Until January," said Fiona.

Everyone stopped eating. Charlie sat with her mouth full of food half chewed hanging open.

"Charlie, close your mouth and swallow," said Fiona.

"Tell her no," said Al unconcernedly when no one else could think of anything to say. He took another piece of French bread out of the bread basket and mopped his plate with it.

"We can't," said Fiona. "We owe her."

"Big-time," said Marlin. "Besides, she didn't ask. She stated it like a fact."

"You don't owe her a three-month visit. Nobody owes anyone that," said Al, leaning back in his chair and stretching. "Good lasagna, Marl."

Marl was Fiona's special nickname for Marlin and she objected when Al used it but over the course of the summer had given up. All of them had had to make adjustments.

And with that he pushed his chair out and stood to make his way back to his trailer.

"Where will she sleep?" asked Natasha. "She's not sleeping in Charlie's and my room."

"That is the question," said Fiona, sighing.

"Maybe she can sleep in the bathroom," said Charlie helpfully.

Martha's house had an enormous bathroom. So big that it housed both a washstand and a big dresser where Natalie and Charlie kept their clothes.

Al had explained that when the house was built in the 1800s it had no indoor plumbing. It had an outhouse and a big hand pump outside. When one of the subsequent owners put in an indoor bathroom they converted one of the bedrooms upstairs, which was why it was so large. The girls loved this quirky bathroom. Even though one bathroom and four girls was not ideal, they all thought taking baths in such a huge room made up for it.

"Maybe she can sleep in the old horse shelter," called Al over his shoulder in parting.

"Can we put Aunt Martha's bed there?" asked Charlie, who didn't always recognize a joke.

"No," said Fiona, her mind scurrying to figure out how to accommodate Mrs. Weatherspoon. "Anyway, Al sold it for us on Used St. Mary's, remember? We only have the four cots now so I don't know what we're going to do."

"Can *we* sleep in the old horse shelter?" asked Charlie.

"No," said Fiona. "Let me think."

She went over to the couch and put her head in her hands. Three whole months. Aunt Martha's house had been big enough for Aunt Martha and was just big enough for the four McCready sisters. There was a kitchen open to the dining area with its big farm table, a living room with a couch and TV, and Aunt Martha's office, which was entirely taken up by her desk and bookshelves. Upstairs were two bedrooms, the huge bathroom, and above those an attic that had a low slanted ceiling, no insulation, and a lot of spiders. Mrs. Weatherspoon was part of the same church the girls had been brought up in. On missions she was used to living in out-of-the-way places, as were the girls, in accommodations that were small or lacking, and having to cheerfully make do. And as much as Fiona knew she should just regard Mrs. Weatherspoon's visit in this light, she still couldn't think of any good place to put her. She didn't *feel* like being accommodating. She felt like being cozy with only her three sisters and herself in the house. After such a turbulent time in their lives they had finally settled into their Pine Island home and she didn't feel like having their applecart upset.

By the time Charlie and Natasha had finished clearing the table and doing the dishes, Fiona still hadn't come up with a solution and Al had returned for the nightly *Jeopardy!* game on TV. This was a ritual he had begun. It was something he used to do with Aunt Martha and he had missed it, was a fiercely competitive player, and beat all the girls every night. It was Marlin and Fiona's goal to win against him just once. Tonight, of the four girls, Marlin alone shouted her answers, trying to get them in before Al did, while Fiona stared glumly at the set, her mind only half on the game.

After the younger girls had gone up to bed and Al was leaving, he pulled Fiona over.

"All joking aside, Fiona," he said. "This is a small house. Just say *no*."

"I can't," said Fiona. "We're going to have to buy a bed too. We can't put Mrs. Weatherspoon on the floor."

"Buying a bed after just selling one is nuts," said Al again. "Learn to say no."

"I am," said Fiona. "I'm saying no to you. Mrs. Weatherspoon can come. Even if I could find a nice way to say no to her it would be the wrong thing to do. Can you take me into Shoreline bed shopping? We'll put it in Marlin's and my bedroom and we'll move in with Charlie and Natasha. I don't want to buy a huge bed so I guess we'll buy Mrs. Weatherspoon a twin but she's really a big woman. I don't think that's going to be entirely comfortable for her."

"What about your comfort?" said Al. "Heck, come to it, what about mine? What's she going to do all day anyhow? I hope she doesn't think she and I are going to spend the day chatting."

"I don't know," said Fiona with mounting irritation as Al presented more and more difficulties. "Anyhow she's coming so we may as well worry about all that stuff later."

"Your funeral," said Al, and stormed out, the way he always did when Fiona wouldn't take his advice.

Fiona sighed. It was not the way she had wanted the fresh school year to start.

Mr. Byrne

Later that night while Marlin and Fiona stared out the window at the Big Dipper, which Fiona now thought of as an old friend, for it hung in their window making its way from one side to the other as the evening went by, Fiona read the letter out loud.

Dear Girls,

I have loved the little notes Fiona has written catching me up on your activities. I am so happy things have worked out for you. Alas, things have not worked out quite as well for me of late. When I got back to Australia my dear sister Helen became ill as I have already emailed you, Fiona, and I was fortunate to be on hand to care for her through her short illness. But sadly she has finally passed. I could not bring myself to write about this in an email, dears. So I'm sorry I am only catching you up now but I'm afraid my generation was brought up believing email is fine for day-to-day information but births and deaths and marriages should still be conveyed on paper. I have tried to be brave but I have to admit I have been feeling her loss greatly and a terrible void in my life where she once was. I am for the first time a bit at loose ends. I know sorrowfully that such grief and loss and vacuum is something you girls are all too familiar with. How we flounder when someone dear to us dies! In short, I do not know what to do with myself. Should I go back to Illinois where Helen and I grew up? Should I go on another mission for the church? Should I take a cruise? Well, I can't afford the latter, I'm afraid. Helen left all her money to the church, which was a wonderful selfless thing to do but leaves me perhaps with less funds than I anticipated. I made her the beneficiary of my will and had assumed she had done the same for me. But we must never assume.

"I'll say," interrupted Marlin from her bed next to Fiona's. Fiona nodded in agreement and read on.

Then I realized that now that Helen has passed I am free to come to help you girls again and ease you into your new school year. I do regret having neglected the four of you so even if this Al you write about is a kind and competent man, he lacks the woman's touch. I was so aghast when you told me of your great-aunt's death, Fiona, and your recent adoption. And I thought yes, those dear little McCready sisters and I can console each other now. And I can shoulder some of the domestic worry. Marlin will surely be glad to hear that once school starts and when I arrive she can leave the cooking to me. I, of course, do not wish to overstay my welcome so I thought rather than stay the entire school year as was my first instinct, I would stay just until January. By then perhaps I can have you organized and back on your feet. After that I would like to travel a bit across Canada. Not far, probably. A budget like mine cannot hope for far. But perhaps at least as far as Saskatchewan. I have a yen for train travel. The train through the Rockies has always been on my small and modest bucket list. Christmas has always been a special time of year for me and will be a sad one without dear Helen so I will be glad to have the four, well, we must include the new gentleman in your life, mustn't we, I should say the five of you to spend it with.

Best of everything to all of you. Do let me know when you receive this so I can immediately purchase my ticket. I'm afraid the cost of a ticket to Canada from Australia is dreadfully expensive. I would like

*to start looking for a deal on the internet as soon
as you give me the green light. If I can find a Super
Saver, I shall probably arrive sometime at the beginning of October. Prudently I shall only buy a one-way
ticket. We may end up enjoying and profiting from
this union even more than we now think! And wish
to extend the arrangement!*
Your good friend,
Matilda Weatherspoon

"Good friend!" scoffed Marlin. "It's that extend the arrangement part that really terrifies me."

"She *was* a good friend," said Fiona. "She put her life on hold for a whole year to sort us out."

"What kind of good friend invites herself to be a houseguest for, oh, three *months* or so? With option to extend?"

"She thinks she's helping," said Fiona. "I think she may be one of those people who always has to be helping someone. I suppose that's what makes one want to do missionary work. Remember how she told us she nursed her husband through his long illness, then she helped us, then she nursed her sister, now she wants to help us again."

"She does not. She said herself she's at loose ends. She just wants to use *us* to fill her empty hours."

"Maybe in part…" said Fiona.

"*One-way* ticket!" said Marlin. "Did you catch that gem? I guess that's in case she chooses to exercise her extension option?"

"She probably was just thinking..." began Fiona, but she couldn't think just what Mrs. Weatherspoon was thinking.

"What is this about *including* the new gentleman? She acts like she belongs with us and *Al* is the interloper."

"I don't think she means it that way."

"And what's that bit about lacking a woman's touch? That's sexism. Women can be just as sexist as men."

"You don't have to take all her opinions to heart, Marlin," said Fiona.

"It's none of it her business. It's not even her business if we're healthy anymore, it's Al's."

"Oh, for heaven's sake, Marlin, she was just being kind. You act like now that we don't need her we are free to dislike her."

"Why are you defending her?"

"I'm not. Listen, no one wants her here less than I do. I'm just saying it would be awful when she gave up a year of her life for us, not to be willing to shift a bit to help out now that she needs it."

"Where is she going to *sleep*?"

"We'll have to put her in here," said Fiona, rolling over in bed. "There's nowhere else. I'll get Al to take me to

Shoreline and we'll buy an inexpensive cot for her, if such a thing exists. We'll have to move our cots in with Charlie's and Natasha's. The four of us have slept in the same room before."

"I know but now I'm used to it being just us. Charlie goes to bed so early. And you and I can't talk at night like we do now if we have to bunk down with her and Natasha."

"It's just for three months," said Fiona, who was thinking if they had to move out of their bedroom she couldn't watch the Big Dipper out her window every night. What would she be staring at through Charlie and Natasha's window? The shed with the garbage cans.

"Oh, just shoot me now," said Marlin. She had been repeating this periodically all evening.

"All right, I get it," said Fiona, who was growing tired of Marlin saying this. "But what can we do? She's a nice person. We can't just say no."

"Why not? Even Al said we should say no," argued Marlin, who felt like being difficult. "Everything was good. We were all getting comfortable again. Things were *settling*. We *deserve* to be settled. Why can't everything just be nice and cozy for a while without any changes or new disasters?"

"Because life isn't like that," said Fiona with the same mounting irritation she'd felt with Al, who wanted to keep presenting problems she couldn't solve. "And if it's not, there's no sense wishing it were." And she rolled over and closed her eyes.

"There's a lot of sense *wishing* it were. There's no sense *believing* it is," corrected Marlin. Then she too rolled over to go to sleep.

<hr>

The next morning the girls waited at the end of their driveway for the school bus. Natasha fidgeted excitedly, wondering if she would get her violin today. Charlie couldn't wait to see Ashley and tell her about Mrs. Weatherspoon coming. Marlin, anticipating finally being able to make a few close friends, mentally scanned the girls from her class last year, trying to decide who was a likely candidate for a best friend. She wanted someone smart and interesting and wondered if there was anyone quite smart or interesting enough for her. Meanwhile, Fiona perfected what she would say to Davy Clement to explain why she had stood him up the previous year. St. Mary's By the Sea Secondary School was small enough that she knew she would run into Davy at some point and she needed to be ready so she wouldn't simply blush and flounder. Her greatest hope was that they could simply pick up where they'd left off without need of much explanation.

When the bus came, the McCreadys piled on and Fiona ran through her speech in her head again and again despite Charlie bouncing up and down in her seat and nattering away in first-day-of-school excitement. Fiona was so wrapped up in her speech memorizing that she hardly noticed the trip to school or the bus filling with children at each stop. She finally came back down to earth as the bus pulled into the elementary school parking lot, where everyone got off, the older kids crossing to the other side of the street where the secondary school was. Marlin and Fiona waved good-bye to Charlie and Natasha, who were headed toward the playground, where their classmates gathered waiting for the bell.

"Bye!" called Marlin to Fiona as Marlin sauntered over to join a group of girls in the parking lot. Fiona vaguely registered Marlin saying, "Well, I spent the summer working on my *book*, of course. I have an *agent*, you know."

When the bell rang, Fiona realized in disappointment that she might not see Davy before school started. She'd hoped to have the speech she dreaded so much over with before the bell rang so that they could arrange to meet outside on an old tree stump for lunch as they used to.

She was sauntering toward the school's front door when she spotted Davy, brushing back the shock of hair that always fell over one eye. His head was thrown back as if he'd just been laughing and his eyes were bright and twinkling. He smiled, and it was this warm smile that had charmed Fiona the preceding spring. But he wasn't smiling at her this time. Davy's smile was directed at the girl who walked pressed into his side comfortably as if she were used to being there.

Oh! thought Fiona. *Oh!* In patting herself on the back for finding a dignified way to deal with an awkward situation it hadn't once occurred to her that Davy wouldn't play *his* part as imagined. Suddenly she felt like an idiot. An idiot! She had thought she was so special—that although Davy might be feeling many things over the course of the summer: angry with her, hurt, longing for her, confused about what had happened—it had never occurred to her that he would have simply *moved on*.

But he seemed to have, for as she went forward his eyes turned once to her and glided away as if she were someone he might have once known but he couldn't really remember.

She scurried forward, putting as much space as she could between them, grateful that he was a year older and wouldn't be in her class. She nipped into the building and went as swiftly as she could to her classroom, where she sat down stunned.

There was an excited hum as students caught up with each other and waited for their new teacher to begin speaking. But Fiona stared at the blackboard lost in her own thoughts. All the contrition and upset she had felt about standing Davy up disappeared as she grew angrier and angrier. How dare he just brush her off like that? It was as if he had simply thought, *Easy come, easy go,* and gone on to the next girl. And who was this new girlfriend? Someone he had known? Well, he should have asked *her* to the dance last June then.

As she stewed over this, her humiliation and indignation mounting, her new teacher introduced himself and Fiona reluctantly turned her attention back to the here and now.

"I'm Mr. Byrne," the new teacher was saying with his thick Irish accent. "I grew up in Donegal, which accounts for the accent, and did my master's in Edinburgh, Scotland, which is where I was living before I came here. Now I'm going to make myself unpopular from the start by giving you assignments on the first day of school."

At this a groan went up from the whole class.

"But I'm going to try not to assign homework for the *weekend* because I well remember what it was to be your age."

A hand shot up and Mr. Byrne answered it.

"How old *are* you?" asked a girl.

"Forty," said Mr. Byrne.

Another hand shot up.

"Are you saying we won't have weekend homework?"

"If you don't finish the assignments you're given during the week, aye, you'll have homework on the weekend, but if you get it all done, well, you get off scot-free. So let's open up the maths book and begin there, seeing as how it's my least-favorite subject. I never was any good at it myself. Maybe you should be teaching *me,* those of you bright buttons who love maths."

A girl raised her hand and Mr. Byrne called on her.

"What *is* your favorite subject?" she asked.

"Oh, English," he said. "I love the poets."

Fiona forgot for a time Davy Clement, Mr. Byrne kept them so busy and she had to concentrate so hard to understand everything he said. She thought the Irish were always redheaded and freckled but Mr. Byrne had snow-white skin and jet-black hair. He wore a rough, baggy tweed jacket even though the day was warm and dress for the teachers at St. Mary's Secondary was usually more casual. Some teachers even wore shorts and sandals through the warm September weather. But it was as if Mr. Byrne dressed out of respect for the subjects he taught, especially English, for which he seemed to have an especial reverence. Fiona was aware she was a more intense person and took things more seriously than most people she met. Sometimes this made her feel as if there were something wrong with her. But Mr. Byrne seemed to have this quality too. When he began on the Romantic poets that morning it was as if he thought they were a window into what life itself was about. He seemed impatient with the students who weren't as fired up about this as he was.

The morning flew by with such an exciting teacher and at lunch Fiona sat with Sarah, who was the girl she knew best from her class, and a few other girls whom she had not gotten to know very well before.

"So?" Sarah asked the table. "What do you think of Mr. Byrne?"

"Cool," said Beth. Beth had come to school looking entirely different this fall. Her hair was dyed light blue and she had a nose ring.

"Very cool," said Carey. "He's definitely something different."

"My mother helped him and his family find a house. He's got two toddlers and his wife is pregnant with a third child," said Megan.

"What's he doing in this hole?" asked Beth.

"St. Mary's By the Sea isn't a hole," said Fiona. "At least I don't think so."

"Well, it ain't exactly a hub," said Beth. "We don't see a whole lot of Irishmen in sports jackets coming through."

"My mother says he's got a father in Vancouver and he's got dual citizenship. He wanted a teaching position in Vancouver but Pine Island was as close as he could get so the family takes the ferry weekends to see the dad."

"Do you think he'll move back to Ireland after this year?" asked Fiona, chewing around the edge of her sandwich and keeping one eye out for Davy.

"Gosh, who knows," said Megan. "It's too bad he's married. He'd be perfect for Agnes at the bakery."

"Have you been to the bakery?" Sarah asked Fiona. "Do you know Agnes?"

"No," said Fiona. "My sister Marlin does all our baking. This is her first year in the secondary school."

"Where is she? Is she in the lunchroom?" asked Sarah.

Fiona looked around and finally spotted Marlin off in the corner eating by herself. She pointed her out.

"She doesn't look very popular," said Beth. "Doesn't she know any of the girls in her class yet?"

"She was talking to a bunch of girls this morning," said Fiona, and wondered what had happened that Marlin was eating alone.

"Oh, look," said Carey, pointing to the front of the lunchroom. "Davy Clement is coming in with Maisie. They were quite the item all summer. They were always at China Beach when I went, draped all over each other. I think it's gross. I mean occasionally they should come up for air."

"Hey," said Sarah, turning to Fiona, "I heard you never went to the dance! I told my sister to watch out for you because you were going to be wearing pants and she said she never saw you there. Or Davy. Did you break up before the dance?"

"We didn't break up. We were never together. Something just came up, that's all, and then I was busy this summer. It was just one of those things." Fiona tried to look unconcerned.

"Gee," said Beth. "Davy Clement invited you to the dance? If he invited me nothing would come up that would keep *me* away. He's hot."

Fiona froze. Davy and Maisie were approaching their table. Anger boiled up within Fiona again.

"Hi, Davy. Hi, Maisie," said Beth.

"Hi, kids," said Maisie. Davy said nothing. Then they had passed and it was over.

"Wow!" said Sarah. "He didn't even say *hi* to you. It was like he didn't even *see* you."

"Who cares?" said Fiona casually.

"Who says 'kids' like that anyhow?" said Beth. "She's only a year older than us."

Fiona nodded and then lunch was over and the girls went back to their classroom. A second later Mr. Byrne entered. He passed out notebooks and said they had to keep journals. To make an entry, no matter how small, every day.

"I'll take a look at them every day at first while you get the hang of it and then later, collect them just once a week. By writing, you discover what you think, to paraphrase that great writer, Joan Didion," he said. "You've half an hour now to do today's entry."

"Do we have to do them even on the weekend?" asked Beth.

"Even on the weekend," replied Mr. Byrne.

"But you said we wouldn't have homework on the weekend," said Beth. "So already you're breaking your promise. I'm disappointed in you."

Fiona found Beth's flirtatious tone cringe-making. Mr. Byrne was a teacher and a married man with a family. But all Mr. Byrne said was, "Put it in your journal."

"And then what?" said Beth. "We all become better people or something?"

"I don't know if there is such a thing as 'better people,'" said Mr. Byrne. "I think the point may be finding out the person that we really are."

Fiona sat staring at the blank page for the first fifteen minutes of their allotted time and then she wrote:

School begins. I had lunch with several girls. Perhaps we will be good friends. We will be getting a dog soon.

That was all she could think of to say that wasn't too personal because Mr. Byrne, after all, would be reading their entries. For so long she'd been in charge of her sisters and keeping the family together and providing a stable environment for the little girls and part of that was keeping her feelings under wraps. Marlin was the only person she shared with and even with Marlin she didn't share everything.

First Day Postmortem

That evening Al came to the house for dinner for the second night in a row. Fiona was surprised. She knew Al was deep at work writing his novel, which usually meant he didn't want to leave the imaginary world of his words. But that night he came bursting into the house, his hair on end as if he'd run his hands through it, and said, "SO! How are the new teachers?"

He sat down with a plop at the dining room table as the girls bustled around setting it and helping Marlin prepare the finishing touches on dinner. He looked, Fiona thought, as if he could hardly wait to see how their first days had gone, a far cry from the previous spring, when if they knocked on his door he shouted "WHAT?" at them and appeared as if he couldn't wait for them to leave.

"Great. Mrs. Cavendish has got a poodle and she said if we're very good she'll bring it to school for a day," said Charlie.

"Then you can see what poodles are like and maybe get unstuck on smooth collies," said Marlin.

"Al, Marlin won't let me have a smooth collie," said Charlie.

"Don't whine, Charlie," said Fiona.

"And don't tattle," said Marlin. "I didn't say that anyhow. Someone is going to get the dog breed she wants but it isn't necessarily going to be *you*, that's all I'm saying."

"It should be. It was my idea to get a dog, wasn't it, Al?"

"Leave me out of it. I'm just the moneybags," said Al.

Fiona frowned. She knew Al was joking but it was a sore point. She was happy that Al had adopted them but she wished to keep a certain independence for the four McCready sisters and part of that independence was paying for things themselves as much as possible. Al insisted on paying for groceries and the general bills like water and hydroelectricity. And Fiona let him because he seemed so set on it and they both knew that if Fiona kept paying those bills the money the girls had would run out before Charlie was eighteen. The whole situation was new and awkward and they were feeling their way. If Fiona was honest, she wasn't ready to have Al interpose himself too completely in their lives. And finances were sticky. Lately Al had been paying for everything before Fiona had a chance, and as grateful as she was for his generosity, when he referred to himself as the moneybags it annoyed her. He knew it and got a kick out of pressing Fiona's carefully controlled buttons.

"We can pay for the dog or dogs ourselves," said Fiona, frowning at him.

"Can you now, Missy?" said Al, leaning back, tipping his chair onto its two rear legs and putting his hands behind his head. "Because a purebred will cost you at least eight hundred dollars a pup plus vet fees."

Fiona, who had yet to research the cost of a dog, gasped.

"Well, we can get a dog from the SPCA then," she amended.

"Still not cheap," said Al airily. He became truculent and challenging whenever Fiona flaunted this independent streak and the two of them often ended up butting heads over what the other three girls considered unimportant issues of expense.

"Who cares if he wants to pay for things?" asked Marlin once when their printer died and Fiona wanted to find the cheapest one to replace it but Al wanted to buy them a better one. "We're all he's got; why shouldn't he spend his money on us?"

Fiona said nothing more but stuck her chin out, something she did when most determined.

"I don't want a mutt," said Charlie. "Ashley says you should never get a mutt or a rescue. You don't know where they've been or what problems they have or anything and they can be bad dogs. You want a purebred from a reliable breeder."

"Oh, a reliable breeder is what we want, is it?" said Al, who was often amused when Charlie used turns of phrase beyond her age.

"That's right," said Charlie. "And a smooth collie is the best."

"Charlie, we're not getting a dog breed just because Ashley likes it best. The next thing you know you'll be giving them names that Ashley picks," said Marlin, putting the baked potatoes and toppings on the table. When things were busy she often made baked potatoes with toppings that they could each dress as they liked.

"I like Feather and Stick," said Charlie.

Al laughed. Then he looked at the little bowls of bacon bits, grated cheese, butter, yogurt, and chopped onion and sighed. "I don't know how you ever got it into your head that a potato is a complete meal."

"COURSES! NEED COURSES!" bellowed Marlin, beating her fork on the table like an imperious king.

"I don't need courses, but if you continue to call one potato dinner then I am going to start ordering out," threatened Al. "What's the point of me buying all these groceries if we're only going to eat potatoes for dinner?"

Fiona frowned at yet another reference to his bill-paying.

Natasha, who had just sat down at the dinner table, got up and said, "Wait, I have something to show you."

She ran upstairs and came running back with her small violin. "See, I got it today."

"Oh," said Al, who had been busy splitting open his potato. "Let me see."

Natasha handed it to him.

He plucked the four strings. "Hmm, sounds in surprisingly good tune. Not bad for an instrument that's been sitting in some school closet all summer."

"How do you know how it's supposed to sound?" asked Marlin.

"I am not completely ignorant of everything," said Al. "They must have tuned them all, Nat, before they sent them home with you."

"Oh, no, it was badly out of tune when they gave it to me. One string was even so loose it almost came off," said Natasha. "I tuned it when I got home." She took it back and plucked the strings lovingly.

"You *tuned* it?" said Fiona. "You haven't even started lessons yet."

"I used the internet," said Natasha. "There's a YouTube video. I'm going to figure out the bow tonight. I don't have my first lesson until two weeks from now so I'm going to take YouTube lessons. Look, I know how to hold it."

Natasha put the violin under her chin and spread her fingers over the handle of the bow. Then she drew the bow slowly across the strings, making the violin squeal.

"Oh, God," said Marlin, "I suppose it's going to sound like cats dying around here from now on."

Natasha ignored her and ran to her room to put the violin carefully back in its case before she began her dinner.

"You don't mind me paying for *that*," said Al sotto voce to Fiona.

"Thank you. I've already said thank you. Natasha has already said thank you. But if you want me to say it again then once again, we're all very grateful," said Fiona.

"Oh, Fiona," said Al, rolling his eyes. "I'm only teasing." Then he took a big gulp of the lemonade Marlin had made. He had already cut his potato into four bites and greedily shoved them down. He rose from the table. "All right, back to work."

"Stop being so mean to him," said Charlie to Fiona.

"Although overworked and underfed on only one small potato like the victim of the Great Famine in Ireland, I know that Fiona is just being Fiona, Charlie, and I take no offense," said Al.

"I didn't get to tell you about my teacher," said Charlie.

"Genius burns," said Al. "I'll come back later for *Jeopardy!* if I finish this chapter and if not, you can tell me tomorrow."

"Tomorrow it will be old news," said Charlie.

"Not to me," said Al, and went crashing out. Then he stuck his head back in and said, "Oh, and Marlin, Steve wrote to me that you've had another rejection. He said to tell you he'd write you a little note tomorrow."

"WHAT?" cried Marlin. "Why did he write to *you*? It's not *your* book. He's supposed to be my agent too, isn't he?"

"He wants to talk to you about it and he didn't have time. He tacked it onto a letter to me. We were talking about something else."

"Well, in the future I'd rather he told *me* first."

"Fine, but don't squawk at me. I'm just the messenger."

"That's what comes from being a teenager," said Marlin. "No one takes you seriously. I wish I'd never told anyone my age."

"Kind of hard to do when you've titled your book *Thirty Meals a Twelve-Year-Old Could Make and Did!*" said Al, and then slammed the door behind him.

"Great," muttered Marlin. "This has just been a GREAT day."

"Why, what else happened?" asked Natasha.

"What kind of pie did you make?" asked Charlie, standing up on her chair and trying to see to the far counter where Marlin usually stored the pies.

"It's in the fridge," said Marlin. "Chocolate cream."

"I want a piece now," said Charlie.

"Wait until everyone is done with their dinner, Charlie," said Fiona, wondering if something else bad had happened to Marlin at school and if that was why she had been eating lunch alone. She figured if Marlin was going to tell her about this it would be later when they were lying in bed and doing their postmortem on the day.

After the girls had eaten their dessert and cleaned up the dishes, Al, who wanted pie, returned and decided to have it in front of the TV with the girls while they all watched *Jeopardy!*

Marlin and Fiona sat on the couch with him and the littler girls lay on cushions on the floor. Natasha liked to lie on her back to watch TV and Charlie usually only sat still for a bit of *Jeopardy!* before getting bored and then switched to marching her fashion dolls around the floor, pretending they were on a catwalk.

"Have you written to Mrs. Weatherspoon yet?" Marlin asked Fiona during a commercial.

"Oh, please tell me you're going to tell that old biddy to peddle her papers elsewhere," said Al.

"I can't," said Fiona. "And please don't call her an old biddy. Charlie just repeats anything you say."

"No, I don't," said Charlie.

"Fiona, you've got to learn to say no to people like that," said Al.

"People like what?" asked Fiona. "You don't even know her."

"I know her type."

"What type?" asked Marlin.

"The type who says she is so sorry that she can only stay three months."

"I've been through all the arguments, thanks," said Fiona.

"Have you thought about the bathroom situation?" asked Al. "Four people and one bathroom is bad enough."

"Maybe she can use yours," Marlin teased him.

"No, thank you, *I* learned to say no a long time ago," said Al.

"We all shared one bathroom with her in Borneo," said Fiona, yawning. "I think we can manage again."

"Well, where are you going to put her?" asked Al. "Have you thought about that?"

"Yes, if you can take me to Shoreline to buy a small cot, we'll put her in my and Marlin's room and we'll bunk with Charlie and Natasha."

"That's a disaster waiting to happen," said Al.

"Do you want to hear about my teacher now?" asked Charlie.

"Yes, that's exactly what I want to hear about," said Al.

"She has a poodle and a *duck*," said Charlie.

"No kidding," said Al. "So her main attraction is her menagerie?"

"Her what?" asked Charlie.

"Zoo, Charlie," said Al.

"She only has a poodle and a duck," said Charlie, coming to sit on the arm of the couch. "That I know of."

As she straddled the couch arm, everyone heard a crack and the arm of the couch suddenly broke off from the rest of the couch and deposited Charlie on the floor.

"Oh, Charlie, I've told you not to sit there," said Fiona.

"This couch is past its prime, don't blame Charlie," said Al. "That arm was already loose. Her weight alone couldn't have done this. You need a new couch."

"We can't afford it. We're already buying a cot. We'll just have to glue it or something," said Fiona.

"People don't fix couch arms," said Al. "They buy new couches."

And then *Jeopardy!* came back on and everyone quickly got another piece of pie and settled in front of the TV and all furniture discussions ceased.

That night as Marlin lay next to Fiona and they stared at the Big Dipper, Marlin said, "I think Al is right. I think it's going to be a disaster moving in with Natasha and Charlie. We'll never get any sleep. Also, can you imagine Al and Mrs. Weatherspoon getting along?"

"He can stay in his trailer for three months if he doesn't like her," said Fiona.

"I wish I had a trailer," said Marlin. "Please can we just make a social excuse? Tell her we all have measles and are highly contagious or something? Maybe we could say Al won't let her come. That would let us off the hook and not hurt her feelings."

"Too late," said Fiona. "I already wrote her an email and said she could come."

"Have you heard back?" asked Marlin.

"Not yet."

"Then there's still hope," said Marlin.

"How was *your* first day?" asked Fiona, changing the subject. "You didn't say."

"Fine," said Marlin curtly. She rolled over. Fiona studied her. Her whole back under the covers was tense. Then she rolled back suddenly. "*You* never told me what happened with Davy Clement. Did you make your big speech?"

"He's got a new girlfriend."

"Yeah, I saw," said Marlin. "I wasn't sure you had. They're draped all over each other all the time. I think it's disgusting."

"Well, anyhow, it doesn't matter so much to me now."

"But still, kind of humiliating," said Marlin. "I mean that he found someone else so soon. So not such a great first day back for you either."

"Well, at least it's over," said Fiona. "You can say that for it."

Then they both rolled away to try to fall asleep but Fiona wondered what Marlin meant when she said not a great day for you *either.* And why she hadn't told Fiona what had gone wrong with *her* day.

Waiting for
Mrs. Weatherspoon

The next day when the girls got home from school there was an email reply from Mrs. Weatherspoon. Fiona read it out loud to them.

Dear Girls,
I knew (well, I hoped) you would be as excited about this turn of events as I have been. I have gone and booked my ticket and will be in Shoreline October 1. I attach airline information. I would leave this very minute if I could but, of course, I booked a Super Saver so I have to wait.
Until then, your dear friend,
Matilda Weatherspoon

"Excited?" said Marlin. "What did you *say* to her? I would have made it clear that I was suffering her to come but only under protest so maybe she'd leave earlier."

"Believe me, I was just polite," said Fiona. "Nowhere did I use the word excited."

"When are you and Marlin moving into our room?" asked Charlie. She was thrilled that all four of them would again be sleeping in the same room the way they used to back in Borneo. Charlie loved falling asleep and waking to hear her three sisters breathing in cots lined up with hers. It made her feel peaceful and safe as if nothing bad from the outside world could happen to them as long as they were a united force, their breaths mingling together all night long in the same room. And having her older sisters close and inert made them seem a little less daunting. A little more accessible and available to her, whereas during the day they often seemed involved in their more mysterious, more grown-up lives that hadn't a lot to do with her. Especially Marlin and Fiona, who were both teenagers now and seemed to be moving away from Charlie to a kind of grown-up existence that Charlie didn't understand and would never catch up with.

"As close to Mrs. Weatherspoon's arrival as possible," said Marlin.

───✦───

Al surprised them that night by deciding to eat dinner with them once more.

Charlie no sooner had filled her plate than she said, "Can we hurry? Ashley is bringing her dog over."

"What?" said Fiona. "Who said she could do that? You don't get to play with Ashley after dinner on a school night. We don't need all that commotion when people are trying to do their homework."

"Yes, so let's invite another body to move in and stay until January," said Al cheerily. "That'll quiet things down wonderfully."

"It's not Ashley, it's just her dog. Her mother said it's a good idea to borrow a dog for a few days before you buy one to make sure it's what you really want. Especially if you've never had one before so Ashley said I could borrow Pebble for three days. And Al said it was all right."

"I thought Charlie would have told you by now," said Al apologetically to Fiona.

"Well, who is going to take care of it while we're at school?" asked Fiona.

"He can stay in the meadow," said Charlie. "It will be like a vacation for Pebble. That's what Ashley and I decided. It's all fenced and there are lots of trees and a shelter. Pebble likes to run. He can chase squirrels all day. Ashley only has a little backyard."

"Wait a second—*Pebble?*" said Marlin. "That's why you want to call our dogs Stick and Feather, right? It goes with Pebble. Jeez, Charlie, can't you be a little original? Do you have to do everything exactly like Ashley?"

Just as they finished dinner, there was a knock on the

door and Charlie ran to get it. Fiona rolled her eyes and went to the door too and Al reluctantly got up to join them. Al was always courtly because he told the girls it was easier to be uber-polite with people you didn't particularly want to have anything to do with than it was to be rude. Rudeness binds you. Politeness creates distance. Fiona thought this was interestingly true and at the same time a very Al axiom. Her parents would have said something more like *Politeness opens your heart, rudeness closes it.* Al's tenets for life were far more pragmatic. And perhaps they were true, because he had spent the previous spring and most of the summer being as rude as possible to the girls and now he had adopted them.

"Hello, Al," said Ashley's mom. "Hello, girls. Here is Pebble. Now, we've brought his food, his dog bed, his bowls, his leash, his ball, and some treats. That should be all he needs for the next few days. You can call me if he is too much. And it's nice of you to let Ashley come over every day after school so that she can visit him."

"Not at all," said Al. "Kind of you to lend him. And her. I can drive her home before supper each night if that works for you."

"Oh, could you? Thanks a bunch. All right, well, it looks like we've come at suppertime, so off we go," said Ashley's mother as Ashley half hid behind her. Ashley was shy around Al, who tended, when there was no grown-up around, to bellow. "Oh, and there's a few little extra things you need to know. Pebble was the runt of the litter and is very submissive. So unfortunately, that makes him something of a piddler. But only if he's nervous. He probably won't be nervous because he knows you, Charlie. Still, this is a strange new place for Pebble, so I would watch him around the furniture. In fact, I wouldn't let him up on any of the furniture at all. Just to be on the safe side. If he does have an accident, try mopping it with plain water. Cleaning fluids or vinegar just makes the spot more interesting and he might pee there again. Plain water, lots of paper towels."

"Will do," said Al, slowly edging Ashley and her mom out the door and walking them to their car while Pebble barked nervously and ran in circles around the house.

Natasha had already gone upstairs, from where they heard the sound of "Twinkle, Twinkle, Little Star" being played repeatedly.

"Turn the volume *DOWN!*" shouted Marlin. "I'm beginning to hate that song."

"I can't turn the volume down, the violin doesn't have a volume button. That's *it*, I can't practice in here," said Natasha, clomping downstairs, ignoring Pebble, and heading out the back door with her fiddle and bow in their case, her ever-present binoculars and the MacBook in her backpack.

"Wait a second, where are you taking the MacBook?" asked Fiona. "And we mean turn the YouTube 'Twinkle, Twinkle' down. We haven't heard your violin, just that stupid YouTube song."

"That is me on the violin," said Natasha in frustration.

"Impossible," said Marlin. "You just got it."

"Just turn the volume down," said Fiona.

"Oh, I give up. I'm going to the horse shelter!" said Natasha.

"Well, come back in time to wash the dishes," said Fiona as she followed Natasha out to the back porch and Charlie chased Pebble around the room. "And don't get the MacBook dirty."

"Yeah, yeah," said Natasha, slamming down the back porch steps and opening the gate to the meadow.

She planned on staying in the horse shelter to try the next song that came after "Twinkle, Twinkle" in her You-Tube violin course for beginners but on the way to the horse shelter she stopped and looked up in joy. The birds of prey were finally gathering. They usually gathered on the northwest part of Pine Island in mid-September and then took off in clouds across the Juan de Fuca Strait, migrating south for the winter. This year they were late because California, Oregon, and Washington were having some of the worst wildfires in history. The birds seemed to know that the smoke hung heavy over the Olympic

Peninsula and were biding their time, late in gathering. But now they had finally arrived—turkey vultures in such numbers they filled the sky. They were high up and circling, riding the thermals as if they hadn't a care in the world. So much motion without sound was hard to process. Nat thought how such a flurry of activity in quiet was so unlike the noisy world that it felt mystical. She stood, her head tilted back, watching in awe. This, she thought, must be what death was like. All life's energy now without physical form. All that energy moving in utter silence.

Without even thinking, she dropped her violin case in the horse shelter, then backtracked to get outside of the fenced meadow and make her way up the trail that she and Al had cut through the forest on the side of the small mountain behind their farm, an almost-straight-up path off which she found the way to the lookout ledge. There, on her rocky ledge, she sat watching the birds that filled the treetops waiting for the secret signal only they knew that meant it was time to fly together across the strait.

The ocean was pink and light blue, a reflection of the sky, the sun beginning to drop into the west and lighting the sky in nursery colors. Nat hugged her knees and wished she'd brought her violin. What would the birds do if she played to them, she wondered, and then she quickly abandoned that idea. So much movement in so deep a stillness, such ancient patterns in the shifting of energies, migrations done time and time again, passed down bird to bird over centuries, didn't need her violin. She lay back on the cold rocks in the surrounding of cavernous time, watching the circling, circling, circling of the birds.

Meanwhile Fiona went back in the house where Pebble was on his back legs, his front legs propped on the dining table, happily eating Natasha's leftover meatloaf.

"Charlie, keep him *OFF* the table," barked Fiona. "And next time tell me before you arrange something like this."

"Al knew," said Charlie.

"Al doesn't live in this house."

"But he's in charge."

"He is *not* in charge, *I'm* in charge!" snapped Fiona.

"Oh, you are, are you?" said Al, coming back in.

"We really didn't need this," she said to Al. "Not on the first week back at school."

"Actually, I think it's a good idea," said Al. "If Pebble, a settled trained older dog, is too much for you, then you may have to rethink getting two puppies, which will be roughly four times the work. And certainly, Charlie should have a chance to see what the reality of having a dog entails."

"Charlie, get him OUT OF THE MEATLOAF!" yelled Fiona. Because now Pebble, having been shoved off the dining table, was putting his front legs on the counter where the meatloaf pan was resting.

"He's not *in* the meatloaf," said Charlie. "He's just licking the pan."

"Even so, Charlie, think about the poor dog! If that pan were hot, he would burn his tongue," said Marlin.

"It's time for *Jeopardy!*" called Al, plunking himself on the couch.

Charlie let go of Pebble to fill the sink with sudsy water so the dishes could soak. Al got up to get himself a piece of leftover chocolate pie.

"This is *great* pie, Marl," said Al.

"Yeah? I think I might do a whole cookbook about pies," said Marlin. "*A Year's Worth of Pies a Twelve-Year-Old Could Make and* Did!"

"You're not twelve," said Charlie.

"Charlie, I already explained why I'm keeping twelve in the titles."

"You should sell the first book before you write the next in the series," said Al.

"Well, that would be nice," said Marlin sarcastically. "But I haven't even heard from Steve. You said he was writing me."

"Don't ask me. He's pretty busy."

"Pretty busy with *what*? I'm his *client*!" said Marlin.

"Yeah, but he hasn't *sold* anything of yours. You aren't making him any money," said Al. "So I doubt if you're at the top of his list. And let us not forget that he is handling this book as a favor and not go all diva on him."

He sat down on the couch and Pebble ran over and jumped up next to him. Before Al could push him off, Pebble had peed copiously all over the couch cushion.

"Oh, *MAN!*" said Marlin, who had been about to sit down herself. "Oh, jeez. That's *DISGUSTING!*"

Fiona ran for a roll of paper towels and a glass of water. She sponged off the couch cushion, which was light gray, and poured water on it. "Now look at it!" she cried. "You can still see the pee."

"Fiona, this couch is done. Between the broken arm and the pee, it's unusable," said Al.

"Maybe so but we can't afford a new one. Marlin, we should put this peed-on cushion on the back porch to air out."

"I don't think it's so bad. Just turn it over," said Marlin.

"Charlie, let's say you and I take a ball and go play with Pebble in the meadow," said Al. "We can record *Jeopardy!* and watch it tomorrow."

"Natasha is in the shelter," said Fiona.

"We won't be anywhere near the shelter, we'll keep to the front of the meadow," said Al.

"Well, warn Natasha," said Fiona. "I don't want Pebble wrecking the MacBook. We *really* can't afford a new one of *those*."

"It's amazing the chaos an extra body can cause around here," said Al. "Maybe you should rethink the Australian houseguest."

"She's not Australian, she's American. She just lives in Australia right now because she's starting up new branches of the church. That's what she does. She recruits and starts new branches. And anyhow, she's booked her ticket. She's coming."

"Just saying," said Al.

"Half an hour, Charlie," said Fiona. "Then bring Natasha in with you. You guys still have to do the dishes."

"She's a hard taskmaster, your sister," said Al to Charlie as they departed with one of Pebble's balls. "Don't forget to record *Jeopardy!*, Fiona."

Fiona set up the recording.

When Al and Charlie got to the meadow they saw immediately that Natasha wasn't in the horse shelter.

"Oh, no!" cried Charlie. "She got lost again!" For Natasha had gotten lost on the mountain the previous spring before she and Al had made the trail. It had been a terrible time until they found her and it had impressed Charlie greatly. Also, Charlie knew from firsthand experience that the woods surrounding them were full of bears.

"Nah, look," said Al, pointing upward at the birds. "I'll tell you where she is. She's gone up to the lookout ledge to watch for the migration. Come on, we'd better find her before Fiona knows she snuck up there like that. We can leave Pebble to run around in the meadow since it's all fenced in."

"I think I should tell Fiona," said Charlie.

"Let's give Nat a break. It will only worry Fiona and make her fussier than she is with you lot. I'll have a word with Nat about telling us before she goes up there."

"I'm tired," whined Charlie. "I don't want to climb all the way up to the ledge."

"Come on, get on the gate and I'll piggyback you up," said Al, sighing.

So Charlie climbed happily onto Al's back. This changed everything. A piggyback ride was fun and suddenly she wasn't tired anymore.

"Faster, faster," she said, bopping him lightly on the head, pretending he was a pony.

"Charlie, if you don't stop that I'm going to drop you and then you will have to walk," warned Al.

When they reached Nat, she didn't notice them at first because she had her binoculars out and was zooming in on the vultures and hawks. When she did notice she jumped guiltily to her feet but all Al said was, "Here, give me," motioning for the binoculars, and he looked and then Charlie looked.

"Any sign they're about to take off?" he asked.

"No, not that I would know what that would look like anyway," said Nat.

"Then come on, we'd better make our way back down, you've got dishes and we don't want her nibs in high dudgeon all night," he said.

Nat grabbed her backpack, Charlie climbed back on Al's back, and the three made their way silently down the mountain. When they got to the bottom, Al said quietly, "And next time tell someone before you go."

"I didn't know I was going until I did," said Natasha.

"Even so," said Al. And that was all they said about it.

Then Natasha retrieved her violin and went inside to join Charlie. While the girls washed and dried the dishes, Marlin made all the school lunches for the next day. Then Charlie set up Pebble's bed next to her own and Fiona checked on the pee-stained cushion.

"Look," she said to Marlin, who was standing in the doorway looking out over the meadow as Fiona examined the cushion. "This cushion is ruined."

"Al is right, we need a new couch," said Marlin.

"Do you suppose that really was Natasha playing 'Twinkle, Twinkle'?" asked Fiona.

"No, are you crazy? She just got that violin. No one learns that quick."

"It's just that she got this strange look on her face."

"That's because she knew we knew she was lying," said Marlin.

"Well, maybe, but the expression was more the one she gets when someone hurts her feelings and she decides rather than confronting them she'll just disappear. And if she was lying her feelings wouldn't be hurt."

"I guess we'll find out soon enough," said Marlin. "We can sneak upstairs tomorrow when she's 'practicing' and see if she's listening to YouTube or if she can actually play that thing. Which I don't for one second believe she can."

"I don't know, I don't like spying on Natasha. She'll think you're playing 'gotcha' and get even more withdrawn. Let's just drop it. Anyhow, we'll just turn the couch cushion over," said Fiona, putting it back down and going inside. "Mrs. Weatherspoon or Al can still sit on the couch. There's room for two and the rest of us can sit on the floor."

"There's room for one if it's Mrs. Weatherspoon," said Marlin.

"Marlin, don't keep saying things like that. Charlie and Natasha will pick it up and you know Charlie blurts things out."

"Well, Charlie and Natasha have gone up to bed. If I can't say everything I'm thinking to you, who can I say things to?"

"True, true," agreed Fiona, but she was thinking, *You don't tell me everything by a long shot, you don't tell me what's going on at school, for one.*

Arrival

Pebbles peed on the floor, peed once on Charlie's bed where Charlie had been told not to take him but took him anyway, and peed on the rag rug in the living room. But the girls still wanted to get a dog.

"Just not *that* dog," said Marlin a few days later when Charlie and Al had left in the truck to take Pebbles home.

"No runts of the litter," said Fiona. "At least none that pee on everything."

September flew by after that on wings of new-starts energy. Everyone knew that the real new year began in September when school started, not in January when the year seemed half finished. *Really*, thought Fiona, *the year should be split seasonally into thirds, not quarters, and the seasons should be the school year before Christmas, the school year after Christmas, and then summer vacation.*

They saw little of Natasha, who was playing with her violin out in the horse shelter as she always seemed to these days. She no longer needed the MacBook to practice because her violin teacher had given her sheet music and an exercise book. Al bought her a music stand that collapsed and could be carried to wherever she wanted.

"I wish you hadn't said that about cats dying," Fiona said to Marlin. "I kind of want to hear how she sounds but now she'll *never* play around us."

"I suppose we'll find out how she sounds soon enough once it begins to rain," said Marlin. "She can't take the violin out to the horse shelter in the rain. I just wish we could put Mrs. Weatherspoon's cot out there."

Fiona was supposed to go cot-shopping in Shoreline with Al. Each evening they made a date to do it the next day after school and each day after school Fiona found herself with too much to do. It was an hour's drive to Shoreline and another hour back home. But Fiona suspected that the real reason she didn't want to go was she was avoiding the whole pending reality of Mrs. Weatherspoon.

"I thought you said you weren't going to have weekend homework this year," said Marlin when Saturday came and Fiona had once more begged off. Marlin had been jealous of what Fiona had predicted would be her free weekends. Marlin not only had homework, she was also redoing her cookbook and researching and sending out queries to agents in case Steve decided to dump her, which was her secret fear. And she had her house chores on top of that. She would have liked weekends without homework too.

"Well, yes, that's what Mr. Byrne said, but he gives us a lot of work during the week, way more than any other teacher I've had, and if it's not done we have to do it on the weekend. So it was a little disingenuous, this business of saying he wouldn't give homework on the weekend. And on top of that we have to do our journal entries and he asks us to elaborate on them after we read his comments and I usually do that part on the weekend so it's a *lot* and the other homework piles up."

"What do you write about?" asked Marlin. "You don't tell him stuff about *us*, do you?"

"Oh, no, at least nothing too personal. Just this and that."

"Good," said Marlin. "Because it's none of his business, our lives."

Fiona secretly agreed. The first day she had handed in her journal the entry was short and to the point. *Today the weather was good. We saw the birds begin to gather for their migration. Al and Natasha cleared more of the trail they made to watch them from the mountain behind our house.* When she got the journal back, Mr. Byrne's comment was *You are writing about what happened but not how you felt about it. Do you know?*

Fiona had bristled at this. She did not think it was Mr. Byrne's place to ask her for her private feelings. So she wrote the second day's entry exactly as she had the first and she got the comment, *If you don't want to write about how you feel then what do you* think *about these things? If you don't know, a journal is a place to find out.*

Yes, I know, she thought. *You just don't know and you're not going to.*

Fiona planned to write the entries exactly as she had been the following days; no one could bully her into revealing more of herself than she cared to. But as she was going out the door one day, Mr. Byrne stopped her. "I don't mean to pry, Fiona, I truly don't," he said. And looking up in his eyes, she saw nothing but kindness there and all her crusty Fionaness melted away.

"I know," she said in embarrassment.

"You just seem to me full of interesting thoughts. The responses you give in class are intelligent and thoughtful and I'm always interested to hear what you have to say about things. But none of this ever makes it to your journal and I'm curious as to why."

Fiona nodded and then scuttled out the door, too flustered to even reply. All the way home on the bus she felt buoyed up at the thought that someone thought the things she had to say were "intelligent and thoughtful." So the next day she wrote, *Natasha plays her violin out in the barn so no one will hear her. This is how Natasha lives her life, in quiet places alone so that no one will hear her.* When she got the journal back Mr. Byrne had written, *That's beautiful, Fiona.*

After that, Fiona tried to find things to please or astonish or impress Mr. Byrne. Hoping to get the comment *That's beautiful, Fiona* again.

Mr. Byrne was demanding and critical of everyone in class and his comments on papers were blunter than the ones from other teachers Fiona had had. He didn't seem to care about anyone's self-esteem. *Avoid the twaddle* was one of his favorite phrases. So to have him write *That's beautiful* was like hearing a bell rung. After that, she was disappointed when her journal didn't come back with such a comment, or came back with no comment at all. And sometimes he said things that got her back up too. On one entry he wrote, *I think you're just voicing a fashionable opinion because you think it makes you look better. Is this what you really think? Think for yourself.* It riled her until she took a breath and realized he was right. The truth of what you really thought was sometimes hard to come by and often hard to voice. It made her take greater care with her journal, trying to delve precisely into what she was trying to say.

Fiona was sitting in Martha's office working on a new journal entry when Al came in and said, "You know this is the last Saturday before Mrs. Weatherspoon comes, don't you? If you don't go to pick out a cot with me this week, she's going to get here next Thursday and there will be no bed for her. While I think that would serve her right,

I know your martyred ways and how in that case you would give up your own cot and sleep on a bed of nails, so to avoid that…"

"Oh, jeez," said Fiona. "It's two o'clock. There will hardly be any time to shop by the time we get to Shoreline and I still have so much to do here."

"I'll go! I'll go!" cried Charlie, who was on her stomach playing with her fashion dolls. Charlie loved trips into town with Al because he always took her to Dairy Queen on the way home. Al and Charlie loved many of the same things: Billy Bear, a bear that had been relocated from their woods that Al and Charlie took expeditions to try to find, Oreos, and Dairy Queen chocolate-dipped cones. Fiona thought Al would make a swell eight-year-old.

"Okay, why don't the two of you go?" said Fiona absently, rewriting the same sentence over and over to make it perfect.

"YAY!" cried Charlie.

"Okay, but no complaining about what we pick out," said Al. "Promise?"

"All right, all right, I promise," said Fiona hurriedly. "Just don't spend too much money and make sure it's a good sturdy one."

"You'll have to trust me," said Al.

"Trust *us*," said Charlie.

"Yeah, okay," said Fiona, thinking *How badly could*

they mess up? One cot had to be pretty much like the next, they didn't really need her at all.

When Al and Charlie got home from shopping, Al went to his trailer to have supper and catch up on his work and Charlie squirmed so much in her chair through dinner that Marlin said, "Jeez, Charlie, what was in that ice cream Al got you?"

"Nothing," said Charlie, and smiled and squirmed some more.

"I know that squirm," said Marlin. "You have a secret. Hey, where's the cot? Is it still in Al's truck?"

"It's being *delivered,*" said Charlie importantly.

"That's the big secret?" said Marlin. "That hardly seems squirm-worthy."

"Well, I hope it's being delivered before Mrs. Weatherspoon gets here," said Fiona.

"It's being delivered *the same day,*" said Charlie. "It's coming after school sometime on Thursday and Mrs. Weatherspoon's plane gets in after dinner that night."

"That's cutting it close," said Fiona worriedly.

On Thursday when the girls got home from school they had a surprise waiting for them. Opening the door and walking into the living room, Charlie screamed, "IT'S

HERE! It's come while we were in school! And look, they took the old one away."

The other girls stood in the doorway and looked where Charlie pointed.

"That's a couch," said Fiona flatly. Where their old broken-down peed-upon couch had stood was a large yellow gingham sofa.

"It doesn't match the room," said Natasha. The living room had been decorated by Martha all in grays and burgundies.

"We didn't care what it *looked* like," said Charlie. "We decided size was the thing."

"Well, size is certainly the thing," said Marlin. "That couch is enormous. I've never seen one that big."

"It's king-size!" said Charlie. "That's what Al said we needed. A king-size couch."

"So we can all watch TV on it together?" asked Fiona. She couldn't fathom Al's reasoning. She wasn't sure she wanted to be squished in with everyone else even if the couch was enormous. And knowing Al, she couldn't believe he'd want to be either.

"Never mind, never mind," said Charlie. "We had a *plan*. And I promised not to show you until Al was here."

She tore out of the house and ran to Al's trailer to get him.

"I didn't say Al could buy a couch. We can't afford this thing, I'm sure," said Fiona worriedly.

"Oh, he'll probably pay for it," said Marlin unconcernedly. "I kind of like it. It doesn't go with the rest of the room, as Natasha said, but who cares? It's cheerful."

At that moment Al and Charlie came bounding in.

"Ah!" said Al. "You've seen it. Now, before you can make a face like you've been sucking lemons, Fiona, we have something more to show you."

"Stand back! Everyone stand back!" shouted Charlie gleefully.

Al moved the armchair from in front of the couch all the way into the kitchen and then he and Charlie did a curious thing. They removed the couch cushions, grabbed a handle, and unfolded the couch into an enormous bed.

"A sofa bed," said Fiona.

"It's ginormous," said Marlin.

"King-size!" said Charlie gleefully.

Natasha went over and sat on it. Charlie started to bounce on it but Fiona grabbed her and pulled her off.

"How could you buy a sofa without asking me?" demanded Fiona.

"In the first place, you promised you wouldn't complain no matter what we bought," Al reminded her.

"Yes, because you said you were getting a *cot*."

"We didn't say that. We said no matter *what* we bought."

"All right, you have me on a technicality. I won't complain," said Fiona. "But we can't afford it. It has to go back."

"I'm paying for it," said Al. "I'm tired of sitting on a couch with no arm and dog pee and I don't care if you sponged it off."

"And Al said Mrs. Weatherspoon could sleep here and you wouldn't have to move out of your room!" said Charlie.

"WOW!" cried Marlin. "Thanks, Al. That's perfect. There's no time to take it back anyway, Fi. Mrs. Weatherspoon gets in tonight. She has to sleep somewhere."

"I suppose Marlin and I could sleep down here instead," said Fiona slowly.

"No, we couldn't," said Marlin. "I'm not volunteering for that and you aren't either."

"Marlin is right," said Al. "The guest sleeps on the sofa bed and if she doesn't like it, she can cut her visit short. That's all there is to it. Trust me, you never want to make your guest too comfortable."

Fiona knew she should argue the point. She felt control of this family slipping slowly out of her hands. But she had to admit that the thing she'd most been dreading about Mrs. Weatherspoon's visit was having to give up her bedroom and privacy. Now, whether she had asked him to or not, Al had solved the problem.

And then she thought of something else. "We don't

have sheets and blankets to fit," she said. "All we have are doubles from Aunt Martha's old bed. We could have made them work for a twin but not for a king."

"We have to leave for the airport in an hour," said Al. "If you want to leave right now instead, then we will have time to stop in Shoreline and get some king-size bedding."

More expense, thought Fiona, who was still determined to pay for the couch. But she didn't say it out loud because she knew it would turn into another protracted argument about who paid for what.

"Let's go," she said finally. "We can maybe get some not-so-expensive sheets and blankets from Walmart."

"Sounds good to me," said Al. "Who else is coming?"

Natasha said she had to practice her violin. Charlie said she didn't want to do the long drive again, she'd just been to Shoreline the week before, so Marlin said she'd stay home with Natasha and Charlie.

"Okay, let me grab my purse," said Fiona. "Oh, and something to eat."

"Never mind, we'll get supper in town. Come on, we'd better push," said Al.

"Where are we going to eat?" asked Fiona as they headed out the door. "We won't have much time."

"Dairy Queen," said Al.

Al and Fiona got into Aunt Martha's old car, which Al had had tuned up and they used now as often as the truck, and they drove into Shoreline. Fiona hustled through Walmart, picking up all the bedding she needed. They grabbed hot dogs and Dilly Bars at Dairy Queen and then headed to the airport.

Al parked the car in the airport lot and they walked into the terminal. The Shoreline airport was so small that there were no Jetways. People deboarded the planes outside on the tarmac. Al and Fiona watched through the window as passengers made their stumbling way down the steps of the plane and then picked their bags up off the rolling cart or looked confusedly to find where they were supposed to go next.

"There she is!" Fiona cried in excitement, forgetting suddenly that she hadn't wanted Mrs. Weatherspoon to come. Here was someone she knew! Here was a tiny piece of their past. "What's she waiting for?"

Mrs. Weatherspoon, having collected her bag from the rolling cart outside the plane on the tarmac, was looking back up the plane steps expectantly.

"Maybe," said Al, "she's decided she's going to get back on the plane and go home after all. Wouldn't that be nice?"

But at that moment a skinny woman, as skinny as Mrs. Weatherspoon was fat, so thin her legs in jeans looked like two sticks and her brilliantly dyed red hair cut so close that her head looked like the top of a wooden matchstick, came down the steps. She and Mrs. Weatherspoon began an animated conversation as the woman grabbed her bag and the two of them began to walk across the tarmac to the terminal.

"It looks as if your Mrs. Weatherspoon made a seat-mate pal on this trip."

"If they were sitting next to each other why didn't they get off at the same time?" asked Fiona. "And why was Mrs. Weatherspoon waiting for her?"

"You got me," said Al. "Anyhow, let's go stand by the door to the arrivals so Mrs. Weatherspoon can spot you easily."

Al and Fiona walked across the concourse. Passengers from that flight were already coming out the arrival doors and being swept into hugs or hurrying purposefully to the baggage claim or outside to get a taxi.

Mrs. Weatherspoon was still deep in conversation with the Matchstick, as Fiona now thought of her, when she came through the doors into the open concourse.

"Mrs. Weatherspoon!" called Fiona.

Mrs. Weatherspoon stopped in her tracks, holding up the people behind her, and scanned behind the barricade until she found Fiona; then she pointed her out to the Matchstick and the two of them proceeded down the hallway to where they could finally be free of the exit barricades and meet up with Fiona and Al.

"Is she going to ask us to give her new friend a ride?" asked Al.

"I don't know," said Fiona. "But it would be like her. She's one of those people who is always picking up strays."

For a second Al looked annoyed; then he wiped the expression off his face and approached the women.

"Fiona, my dear girl!" said Mrs. Weatherspoon, sweeping her into a hug. "How wonderful to see you again. And this must be Al!"

"How do you do," said Al, shaking her hand.

"I must thank you from the bottom of my heart for caring for these dear girls while I was otherwise indisposed," said Mrs. Weatherspoon. "But no fear, no fear, my obligations are fulfilled and I am entirely at your disposal."

"Not at all," said Al. "It's been my privilege."

"And *this*," said Mrs. Weatherspoon, turning to the Matchstick with great fanfare, "*this* is Jo Menzies. My dear friend."

Al shook hands with Jo but Jo paid no attention to him and instead smiled a toothy greeting at Fiona.

"Tildy has told me so much about you," said Jo, continuing to ignore Al. "I simply had to come. Of course, I had to come anyway because I could hardly stay there in Australia *all alone*. Under the circumstances."

"Had to come?" said Fiona, looking suddenly confused. "You didn't just meet on the plane?"

"Oh, *no*," said Jo, stepping in front of Mrs. Weatherspoon, effectively blocking her from the conversation. "I run the church recruiting office from my home in Peoria. Tildy and I have worked together on recruitment *for years* although from a *distance*. I haven't actually seen Tildy for, what has it been? Thirty, forty years? More? We were GIRLS together. Although Tildy liked to do missions with the church and *I didn't*. The food is always so *bad* and you're always being sent places with *bugs* and people who won't understand *English* no matter how *often* you speak it to them. Now where is the baggage claim? I hope my *luggage* has been transferred. They said in Australia that it might not make the flight to Canada but they would *try*. What do they mean *try*? With the amount they charge for these tickets I expect them to do more than *try*. You'd think they could at least keep track of your *luggage*, wouldn't you? Well, we shall just have to see. Look, the baggage carousel isn't even *moving* yet. They haven't even got the luggage into the *concourse*. You'd think with such a *small* airport they could get the luggage out a little *faster*. I mean I understand it in the big airports with the VOLUME, but in these *dinky* ones…"

Jo headed off toward the baggage claim muttering to herself angrily with Fiona and Al throwing looks at each other in complete confusion.

Mrs. Weatherspoon caught one such look and grabbed Fiona's forearm, saying, "My dear, I know I didn't mention Jo…"

"Is she visiting someone on Pine Island too?" asked Fiona.

"Oh, no," said Mrs. Weatherspoon. "That is, yes. You. You see it happened all so quickly."

Jo was busy jockeying for a good position up close to the opening in the wall where the luggage would come out so Mrs. Weatherspoon, while waiting at the luggage carousel for her bag on the far end from Jo, stopped for a moment and said quietly to Fiona, "I knew you wouldn't mind when you heard poor Jo's story. Her husband died after a long bout of cancer and she was so distraught that she simply hopped on a plane, planning to stay with me in Australia, thinking we could comfort each other in our losses. She figured it would be a wonderful surprise when she showed up and it would have been if I hadn't been about to take off myself so when she called from the airport and said, 'Surprise, I'm at the airport,' I was floored. I had to tell her I was at the airport too! I was leaving in an hour for Canada. After I explained, we decided that the best thing was for her to come with me if we could get her a seat. It was that or give her the keys to my apartment and let her stay there alone but she didn't want to do that. Let me tell you, it was a mad dash to get her a ticket and on the plane with me. No time to alert you and I didn't think you'd mind anyway."

Fiona didn't know how to respond. "Yes," she said

automatically while trying to process this new and horrible wrinkle.

Al looked down at Fiona, smiling wickedly, and said, "Good thing we bought a king- size."

"What's that?" asked Mrs. Weatherspoon.

"Never mind," said Al. "Look, the luggage is coming out."

"Oh, thank heavens," said Mrs. Weatherspoon. "Jo's got one of her suitcases! She was so worried. She talked about nothing else for six straight hours. It's a terrible thing to be without underwear."

"I shall embroider that on a tea towel," said Al quietly.

"What?" said Mrs. Weatherspoon.

"Never mind," said Al. "We should move closer to the carousel. Look, some bags are already getting away! Two have returned to the unknown beyond the rubber curtain, perhaps never to be seen again! We must hurry."

Fiona sighed. Finding out there was yet another houseguest had apparently put Al in one of his moods and when he was in one, there was nothing she could do with him. She was just happy that Mrs. Weatherspoon wasn't the type to pick up on such comments. She took everything everyone said at face value, assuming everyone was as good-natured, earnest, and transparent as she.

They collected the luggage and then the four of them walked out to the car. Al loaded the luggage into the trunk.

Jo explained three times how better to arrange it and then shooed Fiona and Mrs. Weatherspoon to backseats, taking the front herself.

"That way you and Tildy can catch up and Al and I won't interrupt you," said Jo.

But it was Jo who talked on and on loudly, giving no one else a chance.

"Of *course*," said Jo, "I couldn't get a *good deal* on my plane ticket. Not at *that* late date. If Tildy had *told* me she was going to *Canada* I might have gotten a much *better deal*. In fact, I'm sure I *would have,* coming up from the *States*! I could have stayed in her *apartment* in *Australia* but I didn't want to be ALL...ALONE! I mean I could have been *ALL...ALONE* in my own *home,* couldn't I have? So I didn't have much *choice*! It's a lot of flying in a *short time*. But I guess I can put up with *that*."

"Isn't the scenery lovely?" said Mrs. Weatherspoon, her soft tones in sharp contrast to Jo's shrill shrieks. "Look at that sunset."

"*I* hardly *know* what time it *is* with all the *jet lag* I've experienced in the last couple of days!" said Jo.

"Oh, yes, jet lag is difficult, isn't it—" began Mrs. Weatherspoon, but Jo interrupted her.

"You don't know the *HALF* of it, Tildy!" she shrieked. "You only went from Australia to Canada! I went *ALL* the way from Peoria to Australia and without a *BREAK* to Canada. *That's* a whole other *level* of jet lag, let me tell you!"

Fiona had never heard anyone who talked as Jo did, screeching the ends of her sentences and generally trying to animate and elevate them to importance beyond the trivial nature of their content. As if you wouldn't notice how banal her thoughts were if she only delivered them with enough pizzazz.

"Yes, you're right," said Mrs. Weatherspoon quietly.

They were all silent in the car after that.

When they got to the farm, Fiona almost laughed as her sisters piled out onto the porch, one by one smiling a greeting and then doing a double take as they spotted Jo.

"Mrs. Weatherspoon!" said Marlin, coming down the steps.

Mrs. Weatherspoon started to head up toward her but Jo ran ahead and got there first, subtly pushing her way in front of Mrs. Weatherspoon. Jo looked down on Marlin, gave a proprietary, condescending smile, and said, "Just call me Jo."

Jo

As soon as everyone got into the house and Al had dropped off all their bags, Jo said, "Now do I have one more? I think you must have left it in the *trunk*."

Fiona wanted to snap, *He's not a porter!* But instead she said, "I'll get it."

"Oh, that's okay, Fiona," said Al. "Don't worry, Fi, it's a workout."

"Oh, do you work out *TOO*?" Jo shrieked. "I brought my hand weights, *just* the *eight-pound* ones. I thought I could find something to *substitute* for the heavier ones. I do *at least* sixty minutes a day…"

Al smiled grimly and made his way outside to the car with Jo following him, doing a running monologue about her workout routines.

"She could have gotten her bag herself if she was going to go out to the car and back like that anyway," Fiona whispered fiercely to Marlin. Marlin looked at Fiona in surprise. Fiona rarely displayed this kind of temper or whispered rudely when others were around.

Charlie had grabbed one of Mrs. Weatherspoon's hands during this and was happily showing her the office and the kitchen.

When Al and Jo returned with the bag, Al said good night and beat a speedy retreat to his trailer.

"*NOW*," said Jo, taking Charlie's other hand and subtly pulling her away from Mrs. Weatherspoon, "now that it's *FINALLY* just the *six* of us... this *is* a little cabin in the *woods, isn't it*? I guess your aunt didn't mind that living *alone, as she did.* Isn't it compact, Tildy? Do the children call you Tildy?"

"Well, if they're going to call you Jo then I guess they should really call me—" began Mrs. Weatherspoon.

Charlie chimed in, "Tildy!"

"Aunt Matilda, I was going to say," amended Mrs. Weatherspoon, smiling affectionately down on Charlie.

"Or even *MOM!*" said Jo explosively.

To Fiona's horror Jo leaned down and grabbed Charlie's other hand. Then, in a theatrically enthusiastic way, she said, "I mean, Tildy, you've *been* like a mom to them. And they can call me *Aunt* Jo."

"NO!" said Natasha, suddenly coming alive from where she'd sat ghostlike on a corner of the big new sofa taking in the visitors in her quiet way.

"*No*?" repeated Jo.

"I think all of us would prefer her to be Mrs. Weatherspoon," said Fiona as calmly as she could.

"It's what we're used to," said Marlin.

"*I'll* call you Mom and Aunt Jo," said Charlie amiably.

"You will not!" snapped Fiona. "That is, we should all use the same names so it doesn't get confusing. And I don't think Mom and Aunt Jo is very respectful either."

"Are you hungry?" asked Marlin, changing the subject nervously because Jo was smiling but looking dangerous and Fiona looked as if she were ready to explode. "I made a shepherd's pie for dinner and there's some in the fridge I could heat up if you like."

"*REALLY?*" said Jo skeptically. "YOU made it? What's in it?"

"Oh, the usual but I always add a bit of thyme, nutmeg, and rosemary and put some..." Marlin began happily. She was always happiest when cooking or recounting what she had cooked.

"No, I mean what is the *protein*?" asked Jo.

"Jo is vegan," explained Mrs. Weatherspoon. "She has committed to it thoroughly. For the sake of our planet."

"And health," said Jo.

"Oh," said Marlin, at a loss.

"Animal products are *so terrible* for you. It's the way we should *all* eat but I realize *some people* just can't commit!" said Jo.

"The shepherd's pie has hamburger and I'm not sure what we have that's vegan..." began Marlin. This was a new one for her. She often made vegetarian meals even above Al's objections but not vegan. She mentally scanned the contents of their fridge and pantry, trying to think what was made without any animal products at all.

"I can make peanut butter sandwiches," said Charlie, who had just learned to do this for her own lunches and was proud of her new skill.

"That's right, we have peanut butter and bread, of course," said Marlin in relief.

But Jo pulled a face and said, "I can't have any gluten *either.*"

Marlin heated up some shepherd's pie for Mrs. Weatherspoon, and Mrs. Weatherspoon sat on the couch as if her legs wouldn't hold her up any longer. Her face was very red and Fiona wondered if she found Jo as taxing as the rest of them. Jo poked about the kitchen only to declare that the only thing that interested her was a banana.

"*Nope,* you have nothing else I can eat," she said to Marlin with a tight smile.

"We can go to the grocery store tomorrow, can't we, Jo," said Mrs. Weatherspoon. "For your special food."

"Yes, we'll have that *Al fellow* drive us," said Jo.

Hearing Al called that Al fellow in such a peremptory way almost caused Fiona to retort angrily so instead she stomped out to the car, where she suddenly remembered she'd left the new bedding they'd gotten at Walmart. Marlin went with her.

Once outside Fiona said to Marlin, "What are we going to do?"

"Kill her?" suggested Marlin. "Or perhaps tie her to a tree outside and let the cougars eat her? *They're* not vegan."

"Well, I don't suppose she's staying three months too. She must have a life. Surely she's only with us for a week at best."

"As soon as we get back in I'm going up to our room," said Marlin. "And closing the door. Thank God Al insisted on buying the hide-a-bed and we have a room to escape to. Can you imagine if we'd taken the hide-a-bed and had no door to close to shut Jo out? Natasha has already gone up to hide in her room."

"Don't you dare go upstairs alone and desert me," said Fiona.

"You can go to our room too. They'll be tired from the trip. And they can make their own bed, surely."

When Marlin and Fiona got back in they found that Charlie had taken Mrs. Weatherspoon and Jo upstairs to see the bedrooms and bathroom.

"What a *big* bathroom!" said Jo. "Now *that's* a room in this *unusual* house I could grow to like. You know, I said to Tildy, I don't think I could stay *long* in a hotel room because of the *SIZE*. Which of these two bedrooms is *ours*? I guess the one where Natasha isn't. She's not lying on one of our beds, is she?"

"Neither room is yours," said Charlie. "Come and look downstairs. I have a surprise."

Charlie loved pulling out the couch. She had done it several times in the store with Al and many times that afternoon while they waited for their visitors to arrive. To her it was still magic. She tossed the cushions off and opened the hide-a-bed for their guests.

"TA-DA!" she said. "It's brand-new! Al and I bought it and it just got here today!"

There was a silence.

"Oh," said Jo. "Who is *this* for?"

"Both of you," said Charlie. "It's really big!" She hopped onto it and started to jump but Fiona ran over and pulled her off.

"Stop that, Charlie," she said. "You'll break it and it's not for you anyhow. It was for Mrs. Weatherspoon, but now, I guess, I mean it's the only spare bed..."

There was another silence and then Jo said, "Oh, but I have *sleep* problems. Especially since *Hugh* died. I really think two of *you* girls would *fit* better on it. Tildy and I can sleep in *your* beds, the ones *Charlie* showed us upstairs. I don't *usually like* a *twin* bed but I think I could make it work. Especially since the arrangement is so *TEMPORARY*. And it would be better for *you too. You would get this nice brand-new bed!*"

Fiona didn't know what to do. She could hardly argue with a guest and a grown-up one at that, no matter how rude the grown-up was being. She was about to say, "All right," when Marlin leapt in.

"I have sleep problems too," she said. "And I have to get up early for school so I really need my sleep."

"Well, Jo, I think it will be okay for one night and then maybe we can talk about it in the morning," said Mrs. Weatherspoon quickly. "Perhaps we can make the switch then."

"One bed, Tildy? For two people?" argued Jo.

Before Jo could come up with any more arguments, Marlin grabbed Fiona's hand and yanked her upstairs, saying, "You come too, Charlie. We're all going to bed. Good night, Mrs. Weatherspoon and Jo. Sleep tight. Don't let the bedbugs bite!"

The last thing the girls heard as they went upstairs was Jo saying, "BEDBUGS? Do they have *BEDBUGS*?"

⸻

The first thing Marlin heard when she got up the next morning was Jo complaining about the sleeping arrangements in loud tones to Mrs. Weatherspoon, who was making muffled trying-to-sleep sounds in reply.

"I really think the girls should take the couch, Tildy," Jo went on.

"No, dear, I've thought about it and I don't feel right putting those girls out of their own beds. And the cots look very narrow to me. I can see they might fit you but I require a bit more room."

"Perhaps that small one, Charlie, could sleep down here with you and then I could take her bed and we could move that other one, Natasha, in with her sisters."

"I must put my foot down, Jo," said Mrs. Weatherspoon, sounding beleaguered. "Why don't we just pretend we are camping out as we did when we were Girl Scouts."

"Humph," said Jo. "If my back goes out I will have to lay the blame at your doorstep."

"All right, dear," said Mrs. Weatherspoon groggily.

It was uncomfortable going downstairs to find a relative stranger sitting at their table drinking water and lemon and telling Fiona, who had gotten downstairs first, that she was too young for coffee when she tried to make it and pour herself her usual cup. At this Mrs. Weatherspoon, who seemed extremely jet-lagged, lifted her head from the pillow and agreed. "Fiona, dear, the church frowns on caffeine."

"It's not our *church practice* that concerns *me*," said Jo. "*Caffeine is poison.* As soon as we get to town I plan to buy *decaffeinated.* That's a *lot* of jam." Jo had turned to Charlie, who began each day by smothering her toast in heaps of strawberry jam.

Marlin wanted to say, *What business is it of yours?* but Fiona said first, "Hurry up, Charlie. We're going to be late for the bus."

Charlie choked down her jam toast with Jo watching her disapprovingly. And the girls hustled out the door, leaving Mrs. Weatherspoon and Jo to whatever kind of day they planned. From the look of it, Mrs. Weatherspoon planned to sleep all day.

━━━━

When Marlin got to school she found all the various cliques gathered in the corners of the courtyard. Last spring she had hung out with a group of girls who seemed mostly nice but this year after she arrived and told them about her agent, they seemed less interested in her and she noticed that instead of asking her to join their lunch table as they had in the past, there were a lot of covert glances and whispering and when she took the initiative and asked where they would be eating lunch, hoping to make closer friendships with some of them, they said things like *We don't know* and *It's too soon to decide* and weren't in the lunchroom when she arrived there. Later she spied them outside sitting under a tree in the schoolyard, laughing together. She never asked to join them after that. And she was secretly too upset by the whole thing to join any other group. She had been lunching alone all September. In fact, she had been doing pretty much everything alone all September, pretending not to care, telling herself that she had a cookbook to write; she had no free time to hang around with the other girls.

That had been fine as far as it went but this morning her teacher, Mrs. Dennison, had announced that they were going to do group projects. They were to gather into groups of six and write a play on a theme relevant to current events.

"You have an hour to form your group, get organized with a leader and a secretary to take down the script you write together, and type up the final version. First you must decide on a theme. You may start now," said Mrs. Dennison.

Marlin panicked.

Already some kids were standing up and clumping happily together, talking excitedly. Of course, not everyone rushed to a ready-made group but Marlin would head hopelessly over to a group only to find they already had six kids. Or worse, she would get to a group of four or five and they would say, "Sorry, we're asking Susan." It was horrible, horrible, a nightmare event. And finally, as all the groups firmed up, Mrs. Dennison spotted her standing alone, came over, and said, "Found a group yet?"

Marlin didn't want to admit no one wanted her and be led by the hand like a small child and forced upon some already-established group, so she said, "Oh, yes."

"Which one?" asked Mrs. Dennison patiently.

Marlin pointed randomly across the room and started in that direction but the girl in charge of the group she approached said in a loud and exasperated voice, "No, no, we've already *got* six!"

"Oh!" said Marlin.

In the end, Mrs. Dennison had to lead Marlin to a group after all. It was made up of four girls she didn't know very well and another one she actively disliked named Georgia who resembled a walrus. There was something about her disapproving bossy features that awoke Marlin's combative nature. It always bothered Marlin that Georgia didn't seem to realize how inferior to Marlin she was but instead ruled a little covey of sycophants with her slimy walrus flippers.

"Georgia!" said Mrs. Dennison. "Do you have six in your group yet?"

"We're full," said Georgia.

"Who is your sixth?" persisted Mrs. Dennison.

"Can't we go with just five?" whined Georgia.

Marlin didn't know where to look. One of the girls giggled at Georgia's audacity and Marlin's discomfiture.

"No," said Mrs. Dennison.

"But it's *always* just the five of us," whined Georgia. "Our teacher last year didn't mind."

Mrs. Dennison didn't even bother to reply but turned

to Marlin and said, "There you go, you can be in Georgia's group."

Marlin wondered why it was immediately recognized as *Georgia's* group when there were four other girls in it. She wished she could be in any group other than this one but looking around, she could see that this was the only group left with only five members. She was stuck.

"All right, I guess if we *have* to," said Georgia. "Come on, we're sitting in this corner over here. I'm making Rhea our secretary."

"Why?" asked Marlin, bristling. She was immediately annoyed that Georgia had simply taken on the role of leader and assigned a secretary and that everyone else just followed along like sheep. If they weren't going to question Georgia's automatic leadership, she would. She wasn't some namby-pamby follower to be bossed around by despotic aquatic creatures.

"Because," said Georgia, sighing as if putting up with Marlin was just one thing too many in her busy day. "She's *always* the secretary, okay? Now, I think I know what I want to do. Let's do a play about saving the whales."

"I had another idea," said Marlin. "I thought we could do one about the antivaxxers."

"The what?" said Georgia, making a face to indicate how ridiculous this was.

"You know, the people who don't believe in vaccination."

Georgia made another face. "Who wants to do a play about that?" she said.

"I do," said Marlin.

"You're not even really *in* this group," said Georgia.

"You need to go with what Georgia wants," said another of the girls.

"Why?" asked Marlin.

"Because she always has the best ideas," said one of the other girls. "We all want to do the whales, don't we?"

Everyone else nodded.

"See?" said Georgia smugly. Then she pulled out a notebook and pen from her desk and handed them to Rhea, who wrote *Saving the Whales* at the top of the page.

"Is that the title?" asked Marlin. "*Saving the Whales*?"

"Yes," said Rhea. "That's what I wrote."

"Well, maybe we could come up with something a little snappier. I'm kind of good at titles," said Marlin. "I have a cookbook with the title *Thirty Meals a Twelve-Year-Old Could Make and Did!*"

"We're thirteen," said one of the girls.

"Who cares about twelve-year-olds," said another.

"Well, I made up the title when I was twelve and besides, it sounds better because people don't expect a twelve-year-old to make dinner but thirteen sounds older, so it's better to—" Marlin began to explain.

"We're not doing a *cookbook*," interrupted Georgia

scathingly as if Marlin couldn't understand the simplest things. "This is a play about *saving the whales.*"

"CALLED *Saving the Whales,*" put in Rhea.

"And we didn't want to have you as part of our group anyway," said another girl. "You're always pretending to be some kind of movie star with an agent."

"Not a movie star. Writers have agents too," said Marlin.

"Maybe real writers do," said Georgia, and everyone sniggered.

"I am a real writer," said Marlin.

"And I'm a real rock star," said one of the girls, and they sniggered again.

"If you're a writer, where are your books in the library?" asked one.

"What do you have published?" asked another.

"I'm not published yet," said Marlin. "But..."

She didn't finish because Georgia huddled suddenly with her group and whispered something to them and they all started giggling.

Marlin couldn't believe how rude they were being. Had *none* of them been taught manners? After that she gave up trying to wrest power from Georgia. Occasionally she would try to join in by offering an idea but she was talked over and ignored. Marlin discovered how a group could ostensibly have you as part of it but nullify your existence at the same time. Marlin was invisible to them. Georgia had won and all the sheeplike girls in the group were too stupid to care if they were being bossed around by a walrus.

By the end of the day Marlin was so angry that she didn't even speak to her sisters on the bus ride home and when they got there went slamming into the house. She would start supper and make a pie that she could photograph to go into her new cookbook. Getting lost in cooking was the best way to turn off her fuming brain. Who needed the walrus lovers? She had a kitchen of her own and a project to work on and dinner to get. Those were all real-life grown-up things, not like the ridiculous babylike behavior of Georgia and her little sycophants. And when her cookbooks were published and she became famous around the world, that would show them.

Inside she found Jo and Mrs. Weatherspoon putting groceries away.

"We just picked up a few *odds and ends* to make some *nice vegan* meals," said Jo. "Now, I'll make a mock meatloaf for *dinner* tonight and you'll see how wonderful a *vegan* diet *is for you*. People think they will *miss* animal products but vegan food is *way tastier*. I'd better get busy, *the thing* about a vegan meal is that it takes *much longer* because there's so *much chopping*."

"I was going to make chicken," said Marlin flatly. "And a peach pie. I have the chicken defrosted and a new recipe I want to try."

"Oh, I *can't eat chicken*!" said Jo, as if this settled the matter.

"I need to take photos of my food for my cookbook," said Marlin. "I can't take photos unless I can cook."

"You can take photos of *my meals,* I don't *mind,*" said Jo, smiling ingratiatingly.

Marlin looked for support from Fiona but she had already gone up to their bedroom. Natasha had taken her violin and run out to the horse shelter. Only Charlie was still around. But Charlie had jumped onto a barstool at the island and was kneeling on it asking if she could help chop.

"You're too *young* to chop, Little Angel—" began Jo.

"Marlin lets me," interrupted Charlie.

"But you can *crush* some of these nuts under the *rolling pin,*" said Jo.

"Dear, what do you think about starting a branch of the church here?" Mrs. Weatherspoon asked Marlin as she finished unpacking the last bag of groceries. "I've been thinking that since we're here anyway, it would be a good use of my time. Even in grief we don't wish to be idle."

"Okay," said Marlin, thinking this would keep Mrs. Weatherspoon busy. "Mrs. Weatherspoon, I really *need* to cook."

"Oh dear, I thought you'd be pleased to have a day off," said Mrs. Weatherspoon. "Cooking dinner really shouldn't be the responsibility of a thirteen-year-old."

"I *like* to cook," said Marlin.

"I know *just what you mean*," said Jo. "Do you want to help grind these dried mushrooms? They add a nice *umami* flavor to the mock loaf. Umami is—"

"I *know* what umami is," interrupted Marlin rudely.

She stomped upstairs to join Fiona.

"Is she *always* in such a *bad* mood?" Jo asked Charlie as Marlin went crashing into her bedroom.

"Not always," said Charlie.

"I would *hate* to have a sister with a *temper* like that," said Jo, and laughed her fake forced screechy laugh. "And that *other one* that never opens her mouth. I couldn't stand having such a weird sister either. They're both kind of *antisocial* sisters. It must be really *hard* for you."

"Sometimes," said Charlie. "Can I chop the mushrooms?"

"No, we're putting them in the blender," said Jo.

"Can I blend them? Marlin lets me push the buttons."

"*Does* she? That doesn't seem *very safe,* does it, Tildy?"

Marlin, who could hear this whole conversation through the heating grate upstairs, turned to Fiona, who was doing homework, and said, "I want to kill her. We can't even watch TV with them down there."

"Sure you can," said Fiona, sucking on the end of her pen. "They can't stop you from watching TV."

"I mean watch TV in peace. You'd have to talk to them or listen to them. Jo never stops talking. Listen to her down there. No one can get a word in edgewise. And it doesn't seem to bother Charlie. She seems to *like* it."

"I know, I know, but you know what Charlie's like. She likes anything or anyone new. Anyhow, I'm sure Jo will be gone before long and then you'll get your kitchen back. I can eat vegan for a week if it keeps the peace. Listen, I can't talk about Jo right now. I'm trying to do maths."

"Math, you mean. Since when is math plural?"

"Oh, right. Mr. Byrne is from Ireland and calls it that. I guess I picked it up."

Fiona was putting extra effort into math. She was putting extra effort into all her subjects, not wanting to embarrass herself in front of Mr. Byrne.

Nat came back inside to tell Fiona she was going to the mountain ledge to watch the birds.

"Okay, just take your watch and be back by six for dinner," reminded Fiona.

But at five-thirty Jo called everyone to eat.

"It's five-thirty," Fiona said to Marlin. "Didn't anyone tell her we eat at six?"

"Well, I'll go down and tell her we have to get Nat first. It will take me fifteen minutes to get up to the ledge and another to get down so we'll end up eating at six anyway."

Marlin ran downstairs. "I'm just going for Nat," she called as she went out the back door. Then she flew across the field and up the trail through the forested mountainside. At the ledge she found Nat and Al passing Nat's binoculars back and forth, studying the circling birds.

"When are they finally leaving?" asked Marlin.

"I don't know," said Nat. "I'll miss them. I wish I could sit up there in the trees with them."

"Can't you find a tree to climb?" asked Marlin.

"None of them have branches low enough to get a foot-hold," said Nat.

Al looked up. "Look at the eagles," he said.

Two eagles were circling, going higher and higher, one right behind the other in the spiral upward as if they were in some kind of dance.

"You can tell the eagles from the vultures from the hawks by their wingspread," said Nat. "Look, the eagles' wings are flat, the hawks point up a bit, and the vultures have that silvering underneath."

Marlin looked at Nat's animated face. Here on the mountainside she blended in with the trees, the birds, the ocean, and the sky. Here, her face lost its remoteness as if she had come back into herself from wherever else she was most of the time.

"Come on, I ran up to tell you it's supper."

"I was just about to come down anyway," said Nat.

The three of them traipsed back down the mountain-side. There was a nip in the air.

"It will be the rainy season soon," said Al. "Enjoy this weather while it lasts."

"And the sunsets," said Marlin.

"The sunrises are the best," said Nat. "In the morning when we wait for the school bus, the sun comes up as big as a house over the ocean. It gets light first and then just as the air lightens and you can see, there it is, this huge orange sun rising through the trees."

They tromped on down, crunching the maple leaves that were starting to drop in the forest. By the time they arrived at the door Marlin realized she was starving. But instead of the usual table neatly set with good kitchen smells and everyone ready to sit down together they found Fiona sitting uncomfortably with Jo, Mrs. Weatherspoon, and Charlie and the serving dishes half empty and dinner already consumed by the four of them.

"We didn't think we should wait," said Jo. "I didn't want dinner to get *cold*. I didn't think it was *fair* to Charlie or Fiona that you were late for dinner."

Al said nothing except, "What's this?" And looked at the rest of the mock meatloaf on the table.

"It's a mock meatloaf, lentils and brown rice and nutritional yeast..."

Al nodded, turned on his heel, and went back to his trailer.

"Doesn't he want any dinner?" asked Jo. "I find *that* odd. Do you think he's ILL? He's a *very strange* man, isn't he?"

"He keeps food in his trailer," said Fiona. "Cheese and crackers and baked beans and stuff. Sometimes he eats there." She didn't add, *if he doesn't like what Marlin is cooking,* which was rare. Marlin's food always smelled and tasted delicious.

"Well, I guess you girls will want your supper even if you *ARE* late," said Jo. "We'll sit here with you to keep you company."

Nat sat down, looking confused and upset, and Fiona passed her the meatloaf and green beans. Nat put some on her plate and ate it without lifting her eyes. Fiona knew Nat was worried she was being blamed somehow for the tense atmosphere when, really, she had come back for dinner at the time she was supposed to. No one had told her the dinnertime had been changed.

Marlin tasted her meatloaf. It was terrible. She didn't mind meatless meals but it was clear to her that Jo didn't know how to cook. Perhaps she'd been vegan and gluten-free so long her taste buds had atrophied. Marlin looked at Charlie's plate expecting to find her food untouched but she had apparently eaten it all.

"Did you like your mock meatloaf, Charlie?" she asked nastily.

"Yes. Jo thinks we should get smooth collies too," said Charlie.

"We haven't decided about the dog breed yet," Fiona

said to Jo. "It's something we're all going to decide together."

"I remember what it was *like* to be the *youngest,*" said Jo. "You *never* get a *fair voice, do you,* Little Angel? And I certainly don't mind *WHAT* kind of dog you get. Only *I hope* you will get it *after* Mrs. Weatherspoon and I *leave.*"

"Charlie always gets a fair say," said Fiona, trying to keep her tone level.

"*Does* she? That's not what *Charlie* has been telling me."

Fiona now found herself angry with Charlie. Didn't she understand that the four of them had to be a united front against such an interloper?

Charlie saw the look and decided to change the subject. "Jo is going to make a mock turkey for Thanksgiving."

"Yes," said Jo. "I hear Thanksgiving is in October in Canada. Such a silly time of year for it, if you ask me. But don't worry, I can be flexible. If a mock turkey is called for in October, I can bend to the wind."

"No!" said Marlin louder than she planned. "*I'm* making Thanksgiving. I need to for my book but I want to anyway. I have it all planned."

"I'm sure in all the places you lived with your parents on missions, girls, your mother didn't always make turkey," said Mrs. Weatherspoon cheerily. "I bet you've had some different kinds of Thanksgiving meals over the years."

"Is Jo even going to *be* here for Thanksgiving?" asked Marlin of Mrs. Weatherspoon as if Jo weren't in the room.

"Oh, yes, dear, I'll need her to help me start up the church!" said Mrs. Weatherspoon.

Jo smiled toothily at them.

Fiona and Marlin shot each other a look of alarm.

"Well, homework time!" said Marlin, trying to pull Fiona to her feet and upstairs so they could conference.

"Jo said you and Fiona would help with the dishes, Marlin," said Charlie as they started up the stairs.

"Nat and Charlie do those," Fiona said, turning on the steps to address Jo in polite tones.

"Oh, the *littlest* do the dishes?" asked Jo. "Hmmm."

"I cook and Fiona does a lot of other things," said Marlin.

"But you didn't cook tonight, did you?" said Jo.

Marlin, seething, helped Nat and Charlie do the dishes after that and then went upstairs. She wanted to take a bath but Jo was already there showering and when Marlin finally got to run her tub she found Jo had taken all but a dribble of hot water.

"Not a week of her but three months?" said Marlin. "Fiona, what are we going to do?"

Thanksgiving

In the next two weeks the girls' kitchen filled with vegan ingredients. Jo ranted about her pursuit of healthy eating continuously to anyone who would listen.

Waiting for the bus one morning, Fiona read back her recent journal entries. She'd decided to put Jo's rants on paper, wondering what Mr. Byrne would say about her. But as she read her entries Fiona realized she sounded small-minded and petty. Could anyone really be as horrible as Jo? She sounded unreal on paper.

Marlin, who had just gotten an earful of Jo's vegan ideas for Thanksgiving and was still fuming, felt a tug on her raincoat from Charlie, who was hopping up and down and pulling at her.

"WHAT?" snapped Marlin, more crankily than she'd meant to.

"Jo is going to teach me how to make gluten-free rolls for Thanksgiving," said Charlie. "She said we didn't really need any rolls but we'd better make something to pease you."

"Please me?" asked Marlin.

"No, *pease* you," insisted Charlie.

"She means appease you," said Natasha. "I heard her. Jo told me that you were probably an angry person because you can't get along with anyone at school."

"WHAT!" cried Marlin just as the bus pulled up.

"Your teacher called yesterday," said Natasha. "Didn't Jo tell you?"

"My *teacher* called?" said Marlin, grateful that they were the first ones on the bus and there weren't any kids to overhear this.

"Yeah, she wants a conference with Al about your behavior."

"My *behavior*? I haven't *got* any behavior," said Marlin, shocked.

"And Jo said she wouldn't bother Al but would go in for the conference herself as one of the responsible adults. That's what she called herself."

"I can't believe you're telling me this just now, Natasha. Or you, Charlie. Why didn't you tell me right away?"

"I thought you knew," said Natasha, "because you're going to the conference too. Jo wanted it to be just her and the teacher. She said you had a temper and tended to fly off the handle."

"She said *that*? To my *teacher*?" said Marlin. "How *dare* she!"

"But your teacher insisted you come too. So they set it up for this Friday."

"That's *tomorrow*," said Marlin.

"After school," said Natasha. "I guess Jo forgot to tell you."

"Forgot my foot," said Marlin. "Fiona, you didn't know about this, did you?"

"Of course not," said Fiona. "She has no right. She's a houseguest, nothing more. What did Mrs. Weatherspoon say about it, Natasha?"

"She said it was kind of Jo to take an interest."

"Oh, I can't believe how that woman has everyone buffaloed!" screeched Marlin.

"Shh!" said Fiona because the bus driver had turned to see what the commotion was.

Then the bus stopped to pick up another three students and the girls had to whisper.

"Listen, just tell Al. He won't let Jo go in his place to this conference. But what is this *about*, Marlin?" whispered Fiona. "You must have some idea."

"It's nothing. I don't know. I mean there's this girl at school—I can't believe my teacher took Georgia's side. Georgia must have complained because there's no way for Mrs. Dennison to know we didn't get along otherwise."

"Georgia's side about what?" whispered Fiona.

"Never mind. It's too stupid."

"Well, tell Al, that's my advice," said Fiona. "He'll go. It's none of Jo's business."

But Marlin sat slumped in her seat, unable to comprehend how things had come to this pass. She didn't want Jo to go to the conference. But she didn't want Al to either. Al thought a lot of her. She couldn't stand being humiliated in front of him even if he did take her side. Maybe she could get Mrs. Weatherspoon to go. She wouldn't mind that. She would ask her that night.

And that night when Marlin asked Mrs. Weatherspoon, she replied, "Certainly, dear. I will go instead of Jo. Only you ought to thank her for such a kind offer."

Marlin gave a sickly smile and as Jo was standing next to them she turned to her and said, "Thanks, but I'd rather have Mrs. Weatherspoon."

"Of *course*. I *understand*," said Jo with a quiet, self-satisfied smile. "I'm *sure* she can contribute more as she has more *history* with your *relationship difficulties*."

I'm not having relationship difficulties, you are, Marlin wanted to shout, but she clamped her lips together.

<hr/>

The next day after school Marlin stayed on instead of taking the bus home. She fidgeted and wished Al had never told Mrs. Weatherspoon and Jo that they could borrow the car whenever they liked. She was sure Jo wouldn't bother going to any conference she had to walk to. While she waited with Mrs. Dennison for Mrs. Weatherspoon to arrive, she wondered why she had to have an adult there at all. Surely her teacher could talk to her alone about Georgia's complaint.

"Mrs. Dennison," she said. "I don't understand why I need to have anyone else here."

"Oh, it's standard practice," said Mrs. Dennison airily. "If a student is having difficulty at school, we like for the parents to be in on it from the beginning so that if things escalate they don't feel like they've been kept in the dark."

"But I don't understand then why Georgia isn't here with her parents too," said Marlin.

"Why would Georgia be here?" asked Mrs. Dennison.

"Isn't she the one who complained?"

"Well, actually, it was the others in the group. On Georgia's behalf, I believe, because Georgia was too broad-minded to register a complaint, but let's just wait for your guardian to come or who is it who is coming? Oh, yes, I have it here, a Mrs. Weatherspoon called to say she would be coming," Mrs. Dennison read from a note she had made. "You do seem to have a lot of adults claiming responsibility for you and your sisters. And what is her relationship to you?"

"She took care of us in Borneo and now she's living with us temporarily."

"Right. Ah, here she is now." Mrs. Dennison stood up

as the classroom door opened but it wasn't Mrs. Weather-spoon who stepped in, it was Jo.

"Mrs. Weatherspoon!" greeted Mrs. Dennison. "I'm Marlin's teacher, Mrs. Dennison."

"I'm Jo *Menzies*," said Jo. "*Mrs. Weatherspoon* had to make an *appointment* with the *chiropractor* because her *back went out*. I said I did not mind coming a *BIT*. Not a *BIT*."

"Well, excellent. And you are another guardian, I believe you said on the phone?"

"I'm a concerned adult in *the girls' lives*," said Jo. "We're *friends*, aren't we, Marlin?"

"Well, it's nice that the girls have so many concerned adults in their lives but is this change of plan okay with you, Marlin?" asked Mrs. Dennison.

"It's fine," said Marlin through gritted teeth because she just wanted to get the whole thing over with.

"Good, then let's all sit down. Now, the reason I've called this meeting is that I've had multiple complaints about your ability to work in a group. This group of girls you've been put with for this project has been together apparently for years and they all know each other. You know, Marlin, it's not an easy thing to infiltrate such a group. But from what I've heard you've made no effort to get along and have subverted many of their suggestions. There's a feeling that you've really made an uncomfortable situation for all. That you're just not making an effort and seem to have taken an unreasonable dislike to Georgia, the leader of the group. They've asked that you be put into another group but I want to know how you feel about switching groups at this point. Would you have equal difficulty in another group? One of the girls said she was actually scared of you."

"SCARED OF ME?" said Marlin.

"Don't *shout*, Marlin," said Jo with her snick snick laugh. "You'll *scare* Mrs. Dennison *too*."

"I just don't know why they would say those things," said Marlin, who was close to tears, so frustrated was she. She was furious with Jo, she was furious with Georgia and the mean girls. She was a fount of fury. Maybe there *was* something wrong with her. "They were mean to *me*."

"Well," said Mrs. Dennison, tapping her pen. "The best solution is for everyone to get along and mend fences. I could speak to the other girls and ask them to make an effort again and let bygones be bygones. In a small school like this you will be with these same girls for several more years. Best to nip this in the bud, don't you think? Sometimes the easiest thing, Marlin, is to go along to get along."

"Non serviam," said Marlin.

"What?" said Mrs. Dennison, startled.

"She's speaking in tongues," whispered Jo to Mrs. Dennison, gripping the arms of her chair in fright.

"No, it's Latin, I think," said Mrs. Dennison.

"Oh," said Jo, looking discomfited.

"It means I will not serve. I mean I will not serve Georgia," said Marlin. "It's what Satan said to God in heaven before he went down to hell."

"Oh my," said Mrs. Dennison.

"You're a little weirdo, aren't you?" said Jo.

"Non serviam," said Marlin again.

"Are you saying you're Satan and this girl Georgia is God?" asked Jo, looking genuinely confused.

Marlin rolled her eyes.

"I don't think that's what she's saying," said Mrs. Dennison. "Marlin, I don't ask you to serve Georgia, exactly, just don't stir the pot."

"Don't you *worry*, Mrs. Dennison," said Jo. "Mrs. Weatherspoon and I will have a *talk* with Marlin. I'm sure she didn't MEAN to be SCARY. Although if Satan is her hero…"

"Satan is *not* my hero," said Marlin in rising tones of exasperation.

"Well, your mentor then," said Jo. "Your dark lord."

"Can you not extrapolate?" shouted Marlin.

"Don't shout," said Mrs. Dennison as calmly as she could.

"She's getting worked up!" said Jo, leaning back in her chair and looking frightened as if she expected Marlin's head to start spinning on her shoulders. She fingered the cross on her neck nervously.

"Oh, for God's sake," said Marlin.

"Are you switching sides now?" said Jo. "Can you *do* that?"

"*Sides?*" said Marlin.

"You no longer want to call on your dark lord?" said Jo. "I mean no *WONDER* those girls are scared. We'll help her *sort out ways* to get along with others. Deny Satan, Marlin, deny! After all, to work and play well with others is a *LIFE* skill, isn't it, and as an added side benefit, gives Satan no purchase. Right, Mrs. Dennison?"

"Something like that," said Mrs. Dennison, who was beginning to look weary of the whole business and as if she was sorry she'd called the meeting to begin with. "What do *you* think, Marlin?"

Marlin wanted to say, *Just put me in another group or possibly on another planet,* but she could see Mrs. Dennison's point. If she was moved to another group the whole class would know something must be wrong with her. It would be humiliating and aggravating that she'd be blamed for something that the other girls had started to begin with.

"Okay," said Marlin. She didn't know what else to say and she wasn't sure what she was agreeing to at this point.

Jo smiled.

"Okay, I'm sure things will resolve now that we've had this little talk," said Mrs. Dennison. "So, onward?"

"Yes," said Marlin.

"No one will serve Satan!" said Jo.

"No, Satan *said* that. To God," said Marlin, making a last-ditch effort to sort out this morass of tangled misunderstood religious quotes and social skills. "I meant I won't serve Georgia. I did not say it to Satan. Or God."

"Well, it might just as easily have been the other way around, mightn't it?" asked Jo.

"No, it mightn't. That doesn't even make sense," said Marlin.

"Does it make sense to you, Mrs. Dennison?" asked Jo, folding her hands in her lap and smiling complacently.

"Not a whole lot," said Mrs. Dennison.

"You see, you're not making sense," Jo said to Marlin.

"What?" said Mrs. Dennison. "No, that's not what I meant."

"No more praising Satan," Jo admonished Marlin.

"I didn't... oh, never mind," said Marlin.

"Right, have a good Thanksgiving," said Mrs. Dennison. "And next Tuesday we'll all return for a fresh start."

Everyone stood up. Marlin marched self-consciously out of the room with Jo behind her.

Mrs. Dennison sighed and went back to work marking papers. Later when the principal came in and asked if she was going to coach one of the sports teams again in the spring, a job Mrs. Dennison heartily detested, she said, "Non serviam." She couldn't help herself. She had been wanting to say it ever since she had heard Marlin say it.

"What?" asked the principal, startled.

"What? Oh, never mind," said Mrs. Dennison, who decided it was one of those things to say that was liberating in theory but not very practical. "Yes, of course I will."

"Well, good," said the principal, who later looked up non serviam and used it herself when her husband asked her if she wouldn't mind unloading the dishwasher while he made dinner. And so did the phrase make its way around St. Mary's By the Sea until everyone had used it at least once and it finally lost momentum and died out. Much like the bottle-cap-collecting fad of the early eighties.

"Dear me, dear me," said Jo in the parking lot. "I had no IDEA you were having so MUCH trouble at school."

"I'm not!" snapped Marlin.

"Well, well, hmmm," said Jo, and she smiled just a bit to herself as if well pleased with her victory.

They drove for a block quietly and then Jo said, "You know, I bet those girls are really mean girls. It's awful—girls your age—it will get better when you get older. You could be anyone, they just need SOMEONE to target."

Marlin felt slightly mollified. Jo now seemed to be

totally on *her* side. She actually seemed to understand and sympathize.

"I really do *feel* for you," Jo went on. "You know, I had similar problems at your age. I think we all did."

Marlin didn't know what to think. Maybe Jo wasn't so bad after all.

They drove the rest of the way to the chiropractor with Jo telling sympathetic stories of all the people she knew who had been picked on at Marlin's age. She parked the car and they sat waiting for Mrs. Weatherspoon.

"Of course, Tildy wouldn't have so much *trouble* with her back if she would *lose* a little *weight*. It's *terrible* for her health, all the things she eats and the *pills she takes*! *Blood pressure, cholesterol, metformin for diabetes.* You know, if the medical world would pay more attention to *preventative* medicine instead of just prescribing PILLS, PILLS, PILLS. But if I bring it up, if I try to HELP her, she just *squawks*."

"Yes, I know what you mean," said Marlin, suddenly wanting to be agreeable because Jo had been sympathetic to her plight a moment before. It was comforting to have anyone, even Jo, make her feel that the two of them were bonded against a hostile world. And to have Jo confiding her concerns about Mrs. Weatherspoon to her made Marlin feel as if she had been singled out because she, like Jo, could see the flawed ways of others from her superior vantage point. Marlin knew she should resist such easy disdain. But someone else was being judged lacking—it wasn't her, so it was like eating too much pie, you knew it was a bad idea but it was vaguely comforting.

"You know, Charlie may be a little *hyperactive*, have you *noticed*? I think there's some things they can do for such children these days although you don't want to get them on *DRUGS* but maybe a change in *diet*. Sometimes *additives* affect children. Really, who gives children *meat* anymore these days? Or *sugar*? And I notice you aren't careful, you and Fiona, about shopping for non-GMO products because no one knows the long effects of *GMO, do they*? And *Natasha* is a little on the *opposite side*, wouldn't you say? Too *quiet*. She ought to be *drawn out* of herself more. And I don't think Al *LIKES* me. And that makes me *nervous*, of course, and the more *nervous* I get the more I *say* the *wrong thing* around him. But I talked to Tildy about him and she said, Oh, that Al is just all about *himself*."

Marlin was about to burst out with, *He is* NOT. *He adopted us when no one else would.* But before she could, Mrs. Weatherspoon showed up at the car. Suddenly Marlin saw Mrs. Weatherspoon in a new light. As someone who would say something mean about Al behind his back. It was one thing for Mrs. Weatherspoon not to see what Jo was but another thing for her to join forces with her. In that moment Marlin found herself hating everyone. Georgia and the mean girls, Mrs. Turncoat Weatherspoon,

Mrs. Dennison for siding with the mean girls, and Jo, who ignited all this hatred within Marlin whenever she saw her.

"So," said Mrs. Weatherspoon cheerily as she got in the car, "everything cleared up to everyone's satisfaction?"

"Oh, *yes*," said Jo. "I think we straightened that Mrs. Dennison out, *didn't we*, Marlin?"

"Yes," said Marlin, hoping that would be the end of it, but Jo instead insisted on going through it all again, only in this version, she and Marlin had been the victims of Mrs. Dennison's bad-tempered accusations and what had become of the teaching profession? This rant occupied the rest of the drive home. But on the way into the house, Jo pulled Mrs. Weatherspoon aside before they got to the porch and whispered in her ear. Mrs. Weatherspoon pursed her lips and Marlin saw Mrs. Weatherspoon eyeing her disapprovingly. She looked about to speak but before she could, Charlie threw open the door excitedly, crying, "Look at what Al got us while you were gone!" She jumped up and down and pointed to the kitchen counter. There sat an enormous turkey.

It immediately cheered Marlin. A small victory. A victory she desperately needed.

Al stood in the kitchen unpacking groceries.

"I was in Shoreline, Marl, getting an oil change and I got you some supplies for Thanksgiving." He lifted cans of pumpkin and evaporated milk onto the shelves. "I know you said you wanted to start cooking after school so I thought there was no sense you wasting time shopping. Where were you? Charlie said she wasn't allowed to tell."

"Charlie…" said Marlin.

"We were at the school listening to the most *worthless teacher*," said Jo, putting a confiding hand on Al's forearm, which he quickly pulled away as if she had leprosy. "Poor Marlin *can't get along* with some crowd of *mean girls who say she* won't even *try* to fit in no matter how hard *they* work to include her so poor Marl is getting all the blame for the *whole kerfuffle.* I'm sure they're all lying, that group of *mean girls,* even if we can't understand why they really *would.*"

As this so perfectly summed up the situation, Marlin could hardly refute it, but there was something wrong with Jo's telling of it.

"I don't understand," said Al. "Why was Jo there? Why didn't I hear about this?"

"Oh, Al," said Jo, laughing. "You wouldn't understand. A girl wants a woman for things like this. Only another female understands how catty girls can get."

"Is that so, Marlin?" asked Al.

Marlin ground her teeth. She didn't want to agree with Jo but how to explain to Al that she hadn't wanted him to hear about this at all? She didn't know what to say so she just looked at him pleadingly.

"Come on with me to the trailer," he said. "I've got writing to do but first I've something to show you."

They stepped outside but once at the trailer Al turned to Marlin and said, "So what was *that* about? I know you wouldn't have asked for Jo's help so how did she end up at the school?"

"It was supposed to be Mrs. Weatherspoon," said Marlin miserably.

"Were you just not going to tell me then?"

"I didn't want to tell anyone," said Marlin. "Jo answered the phone when my teacher called and…"

"Muscled her way in," said Al. "Yeah, I got that part. SET BOUNDARIES. If she muscles in, say no. And what is this about Mrs. Weatherspoon? *I* should have been there."

And for a second Al looked so hurt that Marlin felt doubly terrible. She didn't know what to say so she just looked at the ground.

Al sighed and opened his trailer door, saying, "All right. You've got your Thanksgiving ingredients and I have a book to write."

When Marlin got back in the house, Jo said, "What kind of writing does he do? All alone in that trailer like a hermit. I hope it's not horror stories like that Stephen King. That would reflect a diseased mind, don't you think? Who thinks of things like evil cars that come after people? He doesn't write things like that, does he, living out back in that trailer like some kind of hermit?"

"Novels," said Marlin curtly.

"Oh, *fiction*," said Jo dismissively. "Almost as bad."

"Horror stories *are* fiction," said Marlin.

But Jo went on as if Marlin had said nothing. "I had a friend who wrote nonfiction. He had to *research*. He couldn't just sit about and *make things up*!"

"Well, as a matter of fact, he writes nonfiction too. He wrote a whole book about my great-aunt."

"Uh-huh," said Jo as he if she didn't believe it.

"It was on the *New York Times* bestseller list!" said Marlin.

"Is that what he told you?" said Jo.

At this Marlin's anger became so molten that she felt like one of those science experiments that bubble up suddenly and froth all over the room. You couldn't win with Jo and the more you argued the more she seemed to feed on it and enjoy it. Marlin finally just left the room but that wasn't very satisfactory either. She replayed the conversation over and over in her head for the rest of the day and woke up at night thinking of all the crushing things she should have said. *What am I becoming?* she thought in despair. *I feel like I'm mad at everyone all the time. What is wrong with me? I need to be around no one. I need to be a hermit.*

All the next day Marlin ignored Jo as she made and refrigerated and prepared bits and pieces for the feast they planned to have on Monday. She was surprised that Jo didn't try to elbow her way into the kitchen more. But she ended up splitting cooking time with Marlin in a more or less amicable manner. The turkey was in the back of the fridge. Jo had filled the front of it with various casserole dishes of lentil and gluten-free concoctions to be reheated for Thanksgiving. Marlin wondered who she thought would eat any of these with the real Thanksgiving food before them but she said nothing, happy to avoid Jo completely whenever possible.

For large parts of Saturday and Sunday afternoon Jo and Mrs. Weatherspoon were gone with Al's car. She and Jo had begun the laborious process of knocking on doors in Shoreline to recruit and hand out the pamphlets she had had the church send to them for this purpose.

Natasha said it was wonderful to have the house to themselves again for two afternoons in a row.

"This feels like a real Thanksgiving with the four of us and no houseguests," said Fiona as she and Charlie and Natasha sat on the couch and watched game shows while Marlin served up bits and pieces of tasty things she was putting together for their feast on Thanksgiving Monday.

"Two more months," said Fiona.

"Three, really," said Marlin.

"The rest of October, November, December," said Natasha. "Two and a half."

"Don't you *like* them?" asked Charlie in surprise.

"Well, it's just a bit crowded, is all," said Fiona.

"We were crowded like this with Mommy and Daddy in places with only two bedrooms," said Charlie.

"Crowded with Mommy and Daddy and crowded with Jo and Mrs. Weatherspoon are two different things," said Marlin.

"Well, I like them and Al too," said Charlie.

"We all like Al. Who said anything about Al?" said Marlin.

"Jo said I'm a little angel," said Charlie.

Marlin had to clamp her lips shut to keep from saying, "Jo said you're a little hyperactive." There was no sense upsetting Charlie. If she was immune to Jo's two-faced ways, she was lucky. She wouldn't spin in bed at night the way Marlin did, replaying the day and things she should have said back to Jo. And eventually, surely, Jo would do something to irritate or upset Charlie too and Charlie would twig to who Jo really was. It was just a matter of time.

Jo and Mrs. Weatherspoon didn't get home until later in the evening on Sunday so the girls were even able to entice Al in for a couple of rounds of the *Jeopardy!* they had taped. But at the first sound of the car returning, he fled back to his trailer. By then the girls were ready to go upstairs to read anyway.

"You know," said Marlin as she and Fiona lay on their backs, their heads on their pillows, and stared out at all the stars, "I used to think if only the severe pain of missing Mom and Dad went away, I would be so happy. And now it has, I mean I miss them but the *severe* pain is gone."

"I know what you mean," said Fiona swiftly because she still didn't like touching that particular wound if she could help it.

"But now other things have come about and I'm still not perfectly happy. Now I keep thinking if only Jo and Mrs. Weatherspoon would leave and Georgia would drop dead, *then* I'd be perfectly happy."

Fiona laughed but then she got serious. "I always thought of you as the one in the family with a temper but, Marlin, I have rage I didn't even know about. When I first saw Jo I thought she looked like a matchstick but now I think she acts like one too. Despite my best intentions five minutes after I'm in the same room with her, I'm in a fury. It's as if she is a pit of rage herself and just being with her sets fire to mine. And what makes me even more furious is how she has co-opted Mrs. Weatherspoon. I want Mrs. Weatherspoon back on our team, Marlin!"

"She did stick up for us when Jo wanted to take our beds," pointed out Marlin.

"I know but I can see Jo just taking over Mrs. Weatherspoon's being like some alien creature with mind control.

Why does Mrs. Weatherspoon not see who Jo really is? I can't stand it! Sometimes I'm afraid I won't be able to stop myself and will just start ranting to Jo about how horrible she is!"

Marlin watched in apprehension as Fiona hit one fist into the side of mattress. "Fiona," she said, "this isn't like you."

"I know," said Fiona worriedly in low tones.

Marlin woke up the next morning and went downstairs to have breakfast and begin to prep the turkey. After she moved all of Jo's casserole dishes out of the way, she found the space where the turkey should have been. There was nothing there.

"Hey!" she yelled at large. "Where's the turkey?"

She began madly taking away milk and almond milk and jam and ketchup and everything that could possibly be blocking her view of the turkey but she knew with a sinking heart it was gone. Nor had it accidentally been moved to the freezer. Or the back porch. Or even the office, because in desperation Marlin checked.

"Will someone please tell me what has happened to the turkey?" she shouted from the front porch, the last place she could think of to look.

"Oh," said Jo, coming down from the bathroom. "We took that back yesterday when we went to town."

"You *took it back*?" gasped Marlin.

"Now don't let loose that well-known temper, Marlin," said Jo. "*Yes, we realized* we had *way too much* food. Fortunately, we found the grocery receipt for it in one of the plastic bags so the store would take it back."

This time Marlin didn't even respond. She clomped out to Al's trailer and banged on his door with all her might.

"WHAT?" he said, flinging it open, still in his bathrobe.

"THEY TOOK BACK MY TURKEY!" screamed Marlin.

"Oh," said Al, rubbing his chin. "Well, I'm not coming in for Thanksgiving dinner if all we're having is that vegan rubbish. I hate lentils."

"WE ALL HATE LENTILS!" shouted Marlin.

"Hey, maybe that could be the title of your next book," said Al.

But Marlin didn't find this funny. "*NO ONE* is going to eat dinner if all we have is that vegan rubbish. We have to go into town to get another turkey."

"Right," said Al.

Marlin heard him muttering to himself under his breath as he closed the door to get dressed. When he came out, they got into his car and drove to the small grocery in St. Mary's By the Sea.

But when he and Marlin arrived there wasn't a turkey to be had.

"We can't have a Thanksgiving dinner without a turkey!" wailed Marlin. "And I need it for my holiday book!

I want a photo of me standing next to the whole prepared dinner and how can we have that with NO TURKEY!"

"MARLIN, STOP SHOUTING!" shouted Al. "Look, I don't have time to go into Shoreline. I've got a deadline for a magazine piece and I'm behind as it is. Jo and that Weatherspoon woman will have to go and get a turkey there."

"Will you talk to them? Jo doesn't listen to me and Mrs. Weatherspoon is afraid of Jo."

"She's afraid of *Jo*?" spluttered Al, laughing. "Mrs. Weatherspoon could take Jo with one hand tied behind her back."

"It's not funny. I have to get that turkey in the oven by noon," said Marlin.

"All right. All right," said Al as they drove back to the farm. "I'll speak to them this once but I don't want to be constantly running interference, understand? You were the people who wanted the houseguests."

"No one *wanted* them," said Marlin.

"Well, you were the ones who insisted on them. I tried to tell you."

"I didn't insist. Fiona did. And even she didn't know Jo would come and would be so horrible. And bossy. And do things like take back turkeys on the sly."

"All right. I don't know what I'll say but I'll think of something," said Al, looking grim.

Marlin never found out what Al said. He insisted on pulling Jo and Mrs. Weatherspoon out of the house and into the driveway to keep the conversation private but after he'd gone back to his trailer Jo came into the kitchen and said, "Now, Al seems to have gotten himself into a *real lather*. That man is going to have a *heart attack*, what with his *bad temper* and *excess weight*. Anyhow, to make him *happy* we're going to go all the way into Shoreline and pick up that turkey you keep insisting on."

"We'll get a turkey, dear," said Mrs. Weatherspoon. "All you had to do was ask. Jo said with all the food she made a turkey seemed a little wasteful. We have to remember how most of the world eats and not be greedy."

With elaborate ceremony Jo got her purse and coat and she and Mrs. Weatherspoon left for Shoreline.

At one o'clock with no sign of Mrs. Weatherspoon and Jo, Fiona said, "You know, Marlin, I bet Jo makes sure they get here too late for you to make the turkey. That would be just like her."

But they finally returned at one-thirty.

Mrs. Weatherspoon heaved a bag onto the counter and said, "Now, there's good news and bad. I know it is getting late to put a whole turkey into the oven but you won't have to because the only turkeys we could still find were frozen and no time to defrost them. But we did find these!

Which Jo thought would work so much better given the time constraints."

And with a flourish she took out several packages of turkey parts.

"Was that Jo's idea, Mrs. Weatherspoon, was it?" asked Fiona in fury.

Mrs. Weatherspoon looked at her in alarm. "We thought you would be pleased to have any turkey. We thought we had saved the day. Jo found the turkey parts."

Jo smiled fatuously.

"Let's show her a little gratitude."

Fiona, trembling, left the room and went upstairs, followed by Marlin.

"You can't take a photo of a Thanksgiving dinner with turkey parts," said Fiona furiously to Marlin. "Jo did this on purpose."

"I know," said Marlin. "She wanted to ruin Thanksgiving and she did."

<hr />

Marlin was sullen through Thanksgiving dinner. Charlie was happy. Jo and Mrs. Weatherspoon were merry. Fiona suspected this was because they figured they'd won. It made her wish she could find a way to ruin things for them. But obsessing over that only made her more miserable. It didn't seem fair that *she* was more miserable than the people *making* her miserable. Natasha seemed not to care that it was turkey parts. Al watched Jo and Mrs. Weatherspoon with fascination as if he were storing them up as characters for some future book. Marlin managed to control her tongue all through dinner. But she fumed.

"Is Marlin sick?" Charlie asked Fiona as Al went back to his trailer and the girls started to clean up the mess.

"A bit," said Fiona.

"Do you think it's from eating meat?" asked Charlie. "Jo says meat makes you sick."

Marlin's eyes grew large as she put away leftovers but she still said nothing.

"If anyone is sick, it's Jo," said Fiona.

"What does that mean?" asked Charlie.

"It means, let's get out the Monopoly board. I'll play with you and Natasha and Marlin in your room until bed."

And that's what they did.

In bed that night Fiona tried to calm down.

"Marlin, it's just one Thanksgiving out of many. We'll probably laugh about it next year."

"That's what you say," said Marlin. "Oh, and guess what, the last thing Charlie told me was that she's becoming a vegan."

This provided the comic relief that Fiona needed and she laughed.

"What?" said Marlin. "It's not funny."

"It kind of is," said Fiona, laughing again. "Charlie

doesn't even know what a vegan is despite Jo talking about it constantly and she won't like it when she does finds out."

"We'll see," said Marlin darkly. "I think Jo is trying to get everyone onto her side against you and me. She's got Mrs. Weatherspoon and now she's going for Charlie."

"Oh, Marlin," said Fiona. "She'll never get Charlie. We won't let it happen."

"Just wait," said Marlin.

Fiona was silent, thinking that she was up nights trying to figure out how to get Mrs. Weatherspoon back on their side and wondering if she would really have to add Charlie to the list. How could she make them see what was so apparent to her and Marlin?

"What if she turns Natasha and Al? What if it's everyone against just you and me?"

"I don't think Jo could do that. Especially not Natasha and Al. Natasha is too sensible and Al thinks they are ridiculous. Didn't you see him watch them through dinner?"

"You've seen her in action, Fiona. She's wily. She becomes charming. She becomes your new best friend. She almost got me on the way to picking up Mrs. Weatherspoon at the chiropractor. She's completely capable of ruining everything. She ruined Thanksgiving. She's going to ruin our family. You have to get rid of her."

Fiona lay in bed wide awake with the words *she's going to ruin our family* haunting her the rest of the night.

Halloween

Two mornings later at breakfast Charlie underwent a vegan catechism with Jo.

"So, Little Angel, why don't we drink milk?"

"Because the baby cows are ripped away from their mothers so that we can get the milk," replied Charlie dutifully.

"And are we baby cows ourselves, Little Angel?"

"Otherwise known as calves," muttered Marlin from the sidelines.

"No," said Charlie.

"So what kind of milk do we drink?" asked Jo in syrupy tones.

"Almond milk or oat milk."

"Do you know," said Marlin, "how much water is used to grow almonds?"

"Let's get the bus," said Fiona.

———✦———

For the next two weeks, to keep her mind off "Georgia and the Mean Girls," as Marlin had taken to calling them, as if they were a girl band, Marlin would attend the group meeting with a notebook and pen and although she said she was taking notes on their play, what she was really doing was going through ideas for Halloween cakes. It kept her calm and put her mind in a happier place than running constantly through her list of grievances with them.

This worked so well that even Mrs. Dennison noticed that there was peace again in the classroom. Georgia and the mean girls weren't nice to Marlin but they ignored her so Marlin was able to work on her recipes in peace. As far as Marlin was concerned it was a tie game. On the Friday before Halloween Mrs. Dennison sought Marlin out where she sat alone in the lunchroom. She made a tiny face, a mini-Jo-moue as Marlin thought of it, when she saw that Marlin was alone and then, seeming to shake this off, she sat breezily down across from Marlin and said, "I just wanted to tell you, Marlin, that I see the effort you have made in trying to get along and I applaud it."

ME? Marlin wanted to say. *It's not ME who is the problem. It's not ME who should be making the effort to get along.* But instead she spat out, "Thanks."

"And because of that I wish to reward you and I think I have come up with a very special treat."

"Oh," said Marlin, so surprised she could think of nothing else to say. She looked at Mrs. Dennison expectantly as if she thought she might pull a chocolate cake out of her purse.

"And this is what I came up with," Mrs. Dennison went on. "We have a school paper that comes out once a month, as you know. Only the seniors are allowed to work on it. And there are only so many positions available. But I talked to the editor and she has agreed to add a new feature to the paper. A cooking column. And you are to write it!"

Marlin stared at Mrs. Dennison. "What does it pay?"

"What?" asked Mrs. Dennison.

"Do they pay by the word or by the piece?"

"Well, it doesn't *pay* anything," said Mrs. Dennison, looking flummoxed. "It's a student paper. No one gets paid."

"Then no thank you," said Marlin. "I have to be paid for my writing. I am *not* a dilettante."

"But, Marlin," said Mrs. Dennison gently, "you must know it takes many years and much hard work to become a paid writer. You have to be patient. And this would be excellent practice and a chance to get feedback from other students."

"Why would I want feedback from other students?" asked Marlin. "Do they know how to write? Most of them can barely read from what I can see. No, Mrs. Dennison, I'm not looking for feedback from the great unwashed."

Mrs. Dennison stared at her speechless.

"But thank you anyway," Marlin added politely.

"All right," said Mrs. Dennison. "Okay, well, I'm surprised is all. And please don't call your fellow students the great unwashed. I thought you would be pleased. I thought you would jump at it. And I thought maybe you would meet some friends with like interests."

"I'd rather be eaten by dogs," said Marlin.

"Goodness, you're, well, you're... something," said Mrs. Dennison, searching for and failing to find an adjective. And thus reaffirming Marlin's opinion of critics.

"Professional?" suggested Marlin. "Principled is probably the word you want. Or perhaps resolute."

"Resolute, I guess," said Mrs. Dennison. "But thanks for the choices."

"You're quite welcome," said Marlin.

And they sat for a second, each with her private thoughts, until Mrs. Dennison shook herself gently and said, "Well, at least give the idea some thought. School might be a happier place for you if you had some friends. I mean, just, perhaps," she added. She looked a little afraid of Marlin now. As if Marlin might offer a selection of better word choices the minute Mrs. Dennison opened her mouth.

"Thank you for thinking of us and we wish you luck taking your idea elsewhere," said Marlin, paraphrasing some of the rejection letters Steve had passed on to her.

"Oh, I'm not offering this to anyone else," said Mrs. Dennison, not understanding. "This offer was dreamt up for you alone. I shall have to think of another treat since I missed the mark on this one."

"Thanks, Mrs. Dennison. I appreciate it, I really do, but I don't need any treats," said Marlin, thinking, *I just need my dignity. Now go away before the other students see you talking to me.*

────────────

When Marlin got home Jo was, as usual, in the kitchen, preempting it so that there was no way Marlin could begin a different dinner plan. So Marlin took her homework out to the porch. It was a clear fall day. Too cold, really, to be sitting outside but better peaceful and chilly than warm and driven crazy.

She had begun her math when Al surprised her by coming out of his trailer, ambling over and sitting in the wicker rocker next to her.

"You got another rejection," he said, getting right to it as was his wont.

"Great," said Marlin. "That's all I need."

"No one said it would be easy, Marl," said Al.

"You didn't have anything to do with this job on the school paper, did you?" asked Marlin, for it suddenly occurred to her that her teacher must have been talking to someone to know that Marlin wanted to be a writer. *Was* a writer. Although perhaps she'd gotten that information from Georgia and the mean girls.

"You got offered a job on a paper?" asked Al.

"Student paper," said Marlin. "I turned it down. I don't work for free."

Al considered this for a moment and then said, "Yeah, I would have done the same. How is school going otherwise?"

"I am being bored to death by the mean girls talking endlessly about the Gap opening soon in Shoreline and how their mothers won't take them there because it's too expensive. And how I am not up on the latest colors because I am such a loser. And Georgia just eggs them on. It would be great if there just weren't Georgia. I can't stand her. She makes my life a misery. And Mrs. Dennison is no better. I made a joke about not taking advice from the great unwashed and she didn't catch the allusion at all. Who knows what she thought it meant."

"Edward Bulwer-Lytton. Irony," said Al.

"Yes, but she didn't want me to use it because people who didn't know what it meant or were too lazy to look it up might be offended. So now I am mad at her too for wanting me to pretend to be stupider than I am and wanting me to run with the pack and not use my own good sense. It's cowardly and it's wrong and I'm furious."

"People are the worst," agreed Al, stretching.

"I'd be just fine if there weren't a Jo or a Georgia or a Mrs. Dennison."

"Marlin, there's *always* going to be a Jo and a Georgia and a Mrs. Dennison," said Al, standing up again. And he shambled back to the trailer.

Marlin sat and doodled contemplatively for a while, watching the fall leaves and drawing witches. Al's last remark worried her. If this was true she was always going to be furious and it was exhausting. Maybe she should move to Alaska and live with a sled dog team. Then she went in to set the table.

<hr/>

"What are you girls going to be for Halloween?" asked Mrs. Weatherspoon that night as they sat down to dinner. "I see you have a sewing machine in the corner of the office so I can help with costumes if you like. In fact, Jo and I could take a couple of days off from knocking on doors and put some lovely costumes together."

"Oh, not me," said Jo. "When it comes to costumes I'm *all thumbs.* Little Angel, how do you like your vegan chili with cashew cheese?"

"It's good," said Charlie.

For a whole week since Charlie had declared she was going vegan, the girls were amazed to find that she had actually kept to an animal-free diet. She used oat milk on her Cheerios and took peanut butter sandwiches on vegan bread to school and resisted the desserts that Marlin kept making despite Jo telling her everything in them would kill you eventually. And she ate whatever Jo made for dinner. Marlin had taken to now and then making a separate meat main course.

"So what kind of costumes would you like?" asked Mrs. Weatherspoon, who was eating the vegan portion of the meal and ignoring the meatloaf. Fiona, watching her, frowned. The longer Mrs. Weatherspoon hung out with Jo, the more she became her twin. This bothered Fiona more than she liked to admit to herself. Turning two people in the house vegan was a definite triumph for Jo.

"Yes, Charlie, are you going as a bean sprout?" asked Marlin.

"Ashley and I are going to be fashion dolls," said Charlie. "I'm sleeping over at her house on Halloween and her mom is taking us to the firehall. They have fireworks there."

"So I've heard," said Fiona. "And a bonfire. Wouldn't you like just a little meatloaf, Mrs. Weatherspoon? Marlin makes a particularly good one."

"Oh, no!" said Mrs. Weatherspoon. "I'm so enjoying what I have. Feeling good while doing good!"

Jo smiled.

"And they have hot dogs at the fireworks," said Marlin cruelly. Charlie loved hot dogs.

"Isn't it *wonderful* what you are doing for your *planet*, Charlie, by eating *cruelty-free*," said Jo. "Wouldn't it be *wonderful* if *more people* refused to eat something capable of *feeling* and *thinking*."

"We eat plants," said Natasha. The others looked at her in astonishment because Natasha rarely spoke up at meals when it wasn't just the four girls. "Plants feel and think."

"Hmmmm," said Jo.

"They do," said Natasha.

"What makes you believe that?" asked Mrs. Weatherspoon.

"Because when I'm in the forest I can feel I'm part of its thought," said Natasha.

"*Well*," said Jo. "*That's* certainly a different viewpoint."

Snick snick snick.

To Fiona's horror, Mrs. Weatherspoon caught Jo's eye and made a snick snick snick–sounding laugh herself.

"Would you like to know what I'm thinking right now?" Marlin asked dangerously, turning to Jo. "Would you like to know what thought I'm inside of?"

"No," said Fiona. "I don't think any of us would."

Snick snick snick, continued Jo.

"So," said Mrs. Weatherspoon. "What are the rest of you girls going to be?"

"I want to be a squirrel," said Natasha. "Our class is having a party and we're all supposed to wear a costume."

"Well, hmm, we'll have to figure out that one," said Mrs. Weatherspoon. "I'll see if I can find a pattern and some fabric when we go into Shoreline tomorrow."

"I'm not doing anything for Halloween," said Marlin. "I'm too old for trick-or-treating and too young for the school dance."

Fiona looked down. She knew this was a partial lie. Marlin was still eating lunch alone every day. Fiona knew that Marlin could dress up and go to the school dance but kids went in groups or with a boyfriend or girlfriend. Nobody went alone. She guessed Marlin just didn't have anyone to go with.

"Then you can help us pass out candy and we'll find some good Halloween movies to watch," said Mrs. Weatherspoon.

"Oh, we're not passing out *candy, Tildy*," said Jo. "You might as well pass out *poison*."

"Oh, right, of course, dear," said Mrs. Weatherspoon.

"You have to pass out candy," said Charlie. "That's what Ashley told me or you get your house egged."

"Well, perhaps we can find a *healthy treat* to pass out," said Jo.

"Or those *spider rings* you can get at Walmart," suggested Mrs. Weatherspoon.

"Or maybe my sugar-free lentil cookies," said Jo.

"Please, let's not pass out lentils on Halloween," said Marlin. "We'll end up not egged but lentiled!"

"Get the spider rings!" said Charlie.

"Gee, Charlie, I guess you won't be able to eat any of your trick-or-treat candy if it isn't vegan," teased Marlin.

"I know," said Charlie seriously. "I'm giving it all to Ashley."

"Oh, Charlie," said Marlin, relenting, "don't do that. I was just joking."

"You can always bring it home to us," said Fiona. "Your own dear sisters."

"If you don't mind getting fat," murmured Jo, looking innocently away.

"I've already told Ashley I would give it to her," said Charlie. "And she's giving me her fashion doll's glitter high heels."

"What about you, Fiona?" asked Mrs. Weatherspoon. "Are you going to the dance? Do you need a costume?"

"I think I'll skip it. I'd rather stay home and watch Halloween movies with Marlin anyway," said Fiona. This was entirely true. She had been invited by Sarah and the girls she ate lunch with to go to the dance with them but she had heard that Mr. Byrne was going to be one of the chaperones and she didn't want to be seen by him in some silly, childish costume.

Fiona had begun to write longer and longer pieces in her journal. And slowly the journal had become her friend and Mr. Byrne with it. When she wrote how she and her family had gone by airplane all over the world and how she loved flying, the feeling of taking off and being neither here nor there, he responded with how he loved the things other people didn't seem to like, the little packages of pretzels, the little cup of Coke and ice. His own small space in the plane defined by armrests. Yes, she had written back, the white noise of the plane to sleep to. The moment the landing gear went up. The moment it came down. *Yes!* he wrote back.

She wrote about how she had fantasized all her life about having a family homestead. A home they had grown up in, a home they would always return to. *What would the house smell like?* he asked. *Old wood,* she said, *a slightly leaky furnace, a hot humid tangle of greenery smell, ham. Who would be there when you returned?* he asked. *My parents,* she wrote. *What would the house look like? A lighthouse,* she said, *I have always wanted to live in a lighthouse. Mine would be a farmhouse,* he wrote, *with a big porch. We live in one now,* she wrote. *Lucky you,* he wrote. *Yes,* she wrote, *lucky us.*

How could she bounce around at a school dance dressed as a zombie after such conversations?

October finished brilliantly with orange leaves everywhere. The birds of prey finally left the island, flying in great black clouds across the Juan de Fuca Strait. The whales migrated and almost daily Natasha saw humpbacks and gray whales, blowing or leaping or feeding on the herring balls that were easy to find because seagulls covered the waters above them in noisy numbers. Orcas even made the occasional appearance and sea lions threaded the waters closer to shore.

Mrs. Weatherspoon outdid herself making Natasha into a squirrel and Charlie into a fashion doll.

On Halloween Charlie and Natasha went skipping happily to school. Fiona's only worry was that although Charlie would be sleeping at Ashley's, going to the bonfire, and seeing the fireworks and trick-or-treating, Natasha had nothing planned beyond the party in her classroom.

"Wouldn't you like one of us to take you trick-or-treating?" asked Fiona.

"No, the houses are too far apart and it's too dark. Probably no one will even be handing out candy around us," said Natasha.

Fiona had spoken to several girls at school about this, wondering if Al, who had bought candy for the trick-or-treaters over Jo's and Mrs. Weatherspoon's protests, had bought enough and was told that in the more remote rural areas, such as Farhill Road where the McCreadys lived, no one came trick-or-treating. That the majority of trick-or-treating happened in the streets around St. Mary's By the Sea, where the houses were close together on small lots and the trick-or-treaters could cover a lot of ground on well-lit streets.

"Well, I bet Mrs. Weatherspoon would drive us and pick us up if we took you into town," said Fiona.

But Natasha just shook her head. Even though she had lived with Mrs. Weatherspoon and Jo for a month, she was still shy with them and didn't engage them in conversation if she could help it. So Fiona dropped the subject but she still worried. She knew that Natasha wouldn't enjoy the firehall celebrations either. She hated noisy fireworks and crowds and too much excitement. And she wouldn't watch scary Halloween movies with the rest of them. Fiona wished she could think of something that would be fun for Natasha on Halloween but she couldn't.

On Halloween when Marlin got to school she discovered that most of the kids were wearing the same costume they would be wearing to the dance that night. Only Marlin, a boy named Josh, and a girl named Jeannie came in their regular clothes.

Great, thought Marlin, *another way to stick out like a sore thumb.*

But it was to get worse than that.

Marlin had gotten up feeling unwell, like she'd swallowed an outboard motor. She wasn't sure if this was because she didn't have a costume and everyone would know she wasn't going to the dance or because she worried that she didn't know if it was geekier to wear a costume to school or not to wear one. If it was too many fiber-filled vegan dinners. Or if she was coming down with a stomach bug. But whatever it was, during silent reading time, she shifted position in her chair uncomfortably over and over as stomach cramps seized her. Then suddenly, oh, most horribly, loudly, unexpectedly and unmistakably and publicly, she farted. She had never done such a thing in her life. There was a nightmarish moment when everyone looked about for the culprit and then Georgia and the mean girls started pointing at Marlin, whispering and giggling. By lunchtime it was clear that everyone knew. Then the jokes began.

How Marlin got through the rest of the day was beyond her. She had thought things were bad when no one noticed her or would have lunch with her but now she longed for those days. Now everyone noticed her.

Everyone came up to her lonely lunch table armed with witticisms.

"Had your sauerkraut today, Marlin?"

"Hi, Marlin, we thought we'd come over and have lunch with you, then we realized you might *explode*!"

Marlin's only consolation was that the jokes were childish and made only by people whose opinion didn't matter to her anyway. But they still highlighted the recent humiliation she would rather forget. And worst of all, Georgia made none. She just wore a look all day of happy triumph as if the thing she had been trying to do to Marlin, ostracize her, make plain to all what a loser she was, Marlin had managed to do to herself. Toward the end of the day, Marlin went into a bathroom stall to cry. She tried to press the tears in by pushing on her eyes with the palms of her hands. She knew it would only add to her humiliation to come out red-eyed and puffy but the incident had been one too many out of her control lately and the tears came anyway.

The day, which felt like it would never end, finally did and she got on the bus dizzy with relief to have it over. Fiona didn't ask her what was wrong. Marlin kept her head turned to face out the window all the way home. But halfway home Fiona's hand found Marlin's so Marlin knew Fiona knew. The whole school knew. Marlin could never go back. She would have to go to boarding school in Shoreline, she decided. She didn't care what it cost. She knew there was an expensive one there with riding classes. She could learn to love horses. Maybe she could work as a groom to earn the tuition.

When they reached home, Al, who had bought a pumpkin for Natasha to carve, was waiting on the porch steps with it but Marlin pushed her way past him without saying hello and went up to her room.

Fiona wondered if Al was also worried about Natasha's Halloween. Since Mrs. Weatherspoon and Jo had arrived, he seldom ventured to the house and pumpkin decorating didn't seem like his thing.

"What's wrong with *her*?" Al asked Fiona after Marlin had charged by and Natasha had gone inside to change out of her squirrel costume for jack-o'-lantern carving.

"Do you promise never to let on that you know?" asked Fiona.

"Hard to say before you tell me," said Al.

"Marlin farted in class," said Fiona.

Al didn't laugh. Instead he looked thoughtful. "Those nasty little witches make a deal out of it?" he asked.

"The whole class did from what I heard," said Fiona. "And they made sure that pretty much the whole school knows."

Al sat quietly on the steps for a second, thinking. Then he went into the house and borrowed the MacBook to look something up.

"Ha! Good," he said to himself.

He went to the bottom of the stairs and called up, "Natasha, put your squirrel suit back on. Marlin, come down here. We're going to town. You too, Fiona, if you want."

"I don't think Natasha wants to go to the firehall and the trick-or-treating won't start for another couple of hours at least," whispered Fiona.

"We're not going to St. Mary's By the Sea, we're going to Shoreline," said Al.

"Why?" asked Fiona.

"We're going shopping," said Al. "I've got a little surprise for Marlin."

"What?" asked Fiona.

"You'll see. Marlin! Natasha! Hurry up," said Al.

"What's Natasha got to do with it?" asked Fiona.

"I've got a surprise for her too. Something different," said Al. "Coming?"

Fiona was torn. She was curious to see what kind of surprises Al had come up with but she had a whole essay to do for Mr. Byrne and she wanted to finish it in time to watch scary movies.

"I can't," she said reluctantly. "I've got too much homework."

"Okay, suit yourself," said Al.

"Won't you tell me where you're taking them?"

"Nope. That's my little secret," said Al.

Marlin dragged herself downstairs. Natasha came down looking very apprehensive in her squirrel suit.

"Come on, into the car, we'll carve the pumpkin when we get home," he said.

"I'm never going back to that school," Marlin said. "And I'm not telling Jo and Mrs. Weatherspoon. Because Jo will want me to go back. She likes to see me tortured. But I'm not. I'll do distance ed or something. Maybe the boarding school in Shoreline. But I'm not going back. I've decided. And don't ask why."

Fiona's stomach dropped as she heard this. This was just what she'd been afraid of. And she knew from bitter experience that once Marlin's mind was made up there was no dissuading her.

"Come on, let's hurry," said Al.

"I'm not going anywhere. I just want to lie in bed and eat all the candy you bought for the trick-or-treaters," said Marlin. "No one's coming to the door anyway and if they did I wouldn't answer it."

"How about we drive by that fancy boarding school in Shoreline and have a look at it?" said Al.

"We can't afford a boarding school," said Fiona worriedly. "Let's not even pretend."

"Come on, Marlin," ordered Al.

"You'll really drive by to see it?" asked Marlin.

"You bet," said Al.

"I don't want to go to boarding school," said Natasha.

"I've got something better planned for you," said Al.

"Do I have to?" asked Natasha.

"Yes," said Al.

So Al, Natasha, and Marlin got in the car and drove off with Fiona wondering what in the world had gotten into him.

Fiona was amazed when almost three hours later a happy-looking Natasha and an excited Marlin came in.

Both girls carried bags. Natasha's was full of Halloween candy. And Marlin's bags said THE GAP

"The GAP!" said Fiona. "I *heard* they were opening one in Shoreline. Everyone wants to go there but no one I know has yet."

"No one in my class has either, but it's all Georgia and the mean girls talk about," said Marlin.

Shoreline had a few stores but nothing as exciting or big-city as the Gap. They'd all seen ads for the Gap and the American commercials on TV but none of them had ever been in one. Growing up on the island in Canada meant being constantly enticed by exciting commercials for trendy things unavailable to them.

"What did you get?" asked Fiona in astonishment.

"I got a *whole outfit!*" said Marlin. "Al bought me everything, even really cool socks that match. In the trendiest color, turquoise, because I asked a salesgirl. Georgia is going to be so jealous. That's all she talks about—that her mother said that *maybe* she *might* get something from the Gap for Christmas. Wait until she sees I have a whole outfit!"

"Then you're going to school tomorrow?" asked Fiona in relief.

"Duh," said Marlin, running upstairs to change into it to show Fiona.

"And I went trick-or-treating at the mall," said Natasha. "Every store in the Shoreline Mall is handing out candy. Look at what I got!" She sat at the kitchen counter and spilled it all out and began to separate it happily into piles.

"Unnecessary clothes and sugar. Two things I *don't* need," said Jo, ostensibly to Mrs. Weatherspoon but loudly enough for all to hear. Fiona knew they liked to play a game together on the computer about the Oregon Trail. They were often at it for hours. Fiona wanted to say, *Games about the Oregon Trail, something I* don't *need,* but she knew this would only make her feel as nasty as Jo.

And anyhow, how neatly Al had solved two of her problems, thought Fiona. She'd worried about Marlin and she'd worried about Natasha. He'd taken Natasha somewhere for a Halloween where it wasn't dark or scary, where there were no fires or fireworks or strange houses with strange doors to knock on.

Natasha had always been Fiona's greatest worry. She was quiet and sensitive in ways none of the other girls were and she disappeared into herself in a way that worried Fiona often because she feared one day Natasha would disappear inwardly and simply never make the journey back out again. Having to take on the care and worry about Natasha was the one thing that made Fiona resentful about her parents' death, even though she knew that was illogical and her parents hadn't wanted to die in a tsunami any more than she had wanted them to. In time she'd shouldered this care, understanding that things happened and it was no good being resentful. You had to go forward and do what you had to do. So Fiona always had her antennae up, making sure Natasha was all right, making sure she was still tethered to her, not floating away somewhere none of them could reach her.

"So, do any of you want some lentil stew?" Jo asked, coming out of the office.

"No, thanks, we got hot dogs at Dairy Queen on the way home," said Al.

"Hot dogs!" said Jo in disgust, but then clamped her lips with a show of virtuous restraint, which everyone ignored.

"And here, we got you this," said Marlin to Fiona, coming downstairs resplendent in new turquoise jeans, T-shirt, sweater, socks, and even a new purse. She handed Fiona a Gap bag.

"Wow, thanks," said Fiona, taking a sweater out of the bag. "Wow."

"We got Natasha and Charlie Gap sweaters too," said Marlin.

"I picked out my own," said Natasha proudly.

"Everyone is going to be green," said Fiona.

"That's the plan," said Al. He saluted in high good humor and returned to his trailer looking very pleased with himself.

The next day after school, Ashley's mom drove over to drop off Charlie and her sleepover stuff. Fiona answered the door but Jo swiftly pushed herself in front of Fiona to talk to Ashley's mom in a very proprietary way, not even letting Fiona stand next to her but somehow managing to block Fiona's way to the door.

"It looks like you can put your name down for two smooth collie puppies if the dog becomes pregnant as planned, because they've started the breeding process," said Ashley's mom.

"That's wonderful *news*. The girls will be *so excited*," said Jo. "Of course, I'd already done that. Aren't you excited, Charlie?"

"Is that Natasha playing violin upstairs?" asked Ashley's mom. "Charlie says she's really good."

Fiona listened for a second.

"I don't think what you're hearing is Natasha," began Fiona but Jo, still blocking her from talking directly to Ashley's mom, talked right over her.

"She's not *that* good," said Jo. *Snick snick snick.* "She's only been doing it since *September.* It must be *YouTube.* She listens to that piece *a lot.* Almost *obsessively,* you might say."

"Well, good for her," said Ashley's mom, and left.

Fiona and Charlie went upstairs. Natasha had taken to locking the door of her and Charlie's room when she practiced and Charlie banged on it to no avail.

"Never mind," said Fiona. "Come into my room and tell me all about Halloween."

So Charlie related tales of trick-or-treating and the bonfire and costume contests until Fiona half wished she were Charlie's age and not a sophisticated fifteen and could do all that as well.

"Let's put your stuff in the wash and pack away the costume. You might still be able to get into it next year."

"Oh, no," said Charlie. "Next year Ashley and I are going as a pair of dice. We saw two other girls like that. And anyway, Ashley and I are going to play dress-up with our costumes."

"Uh-huh," said Fiona. She took the fashion costume out of the bag to hang it up and out fell dozens of little chocolate bars.

"I thought you were giving your candy to Ashley?" said Fiona. "Did you forget?"

"No," said Charlie, opening a chocolate bar and popping it into her mouth. "I decided that I'm going to be vegan downstairs and not vegan upstairs."

"Good plan," said Fiona.

"But it's a secret from Jo."

"Also a good plan," said Fiona. "If I keep your secret can I have a chocolate bar?"

"Yes, but not the Dairy Milks," said Charlie.

"Deal," said Fiona.

Fiona wrote the whole vegan episode up in her journal.

———⟶———

Later when she got it back Mr. Byrne had replied, *Keep an open mind. Shouldn't your sister be allowed to try out something new? I know you despise Jo but you must admit she is doing something principled and difficult to help save the planet. And perhaps because she loves animals.*

So she keeps telling us, Fiona wrote back in another of their continuing threads when she returned the journal again. *It isn't what she does, it is how she uses it to condemn everyone else. You aren't there so you can't catch the nuances. You are sitting in judgment of me without even meeting Jo and understanding what she's like.*

Mr. Byrne wrote back, *You are right. I should give you more credit. We can all see some things but we cannot see everything. P.S. I am vegan.*

November

November started out well. Although it rained heavily every day. The island was in the throes of a Pineapple Express, a weather front from Hawaii with heavy warm tropical rain. The girls had experienced this kind of tropical rain before. They were happy listening to it, curled up around the living room and office reading.

Just then Al came tromping in. He took off his muddy boots and shook himself like a dog.

"Mudslide has closed the road between here and Shoreline," he announced.

"Oh, no," said Charlie. "What will Mrs. Weatherspoon and Jo do?"

"They're in Shoreline recruiting church members," explained Fiona.

"For what?" asked Al, who kept to himself in the trailer, avoiding the houseguests as much as possible, and therefore was often not apprised of the latest news.

"They want to start a branch of the church here," said Marlin sourly. "They have eight members and if they get twenty, the church will send them money and find a pastor to move here and they'll rent a hall and get it set up."

"But that will never happen," said Fiona. "At least, I doubt it. It's taken them all this time just to find eight people to sign up. There are only so many doors to knock on in Shoreline."

"How will they get home if the road is closed?" asked Charlie.

"Don't say home. This isn't their home," said Marlin.

"It looks like they're going to be stuck in Shoreline tonight," said Al cheerfully. "I heard on the radio that the road will be closed at least twenty-four hours and maybe more."

"Hooray!" said Marlin. "I get to make dinner."

"What will you make?" asked Al.

"Pork chops," said Marlin, knowing this was Al's favorite. "And mashed potatoes and peas and this new cake I wanted to try with toasted marshmallow frosting."

"Sounds good to me," said Al.

"What about you, Charlie?" asked Marlin. "Will you eat that? Because I think there's some leftover bulgur taco 'meat' I can heat up for you."

"I think I'll have pork chops," said Charlie, looking shifty-eyed.

"Don't worry," said Fiona. "We won't tell."

"And cake," said Charlie.

Marlin went off to make it.

When dinner was ready Al sat down at the table with another announcement.

"I'm sorry, Natasha," he said, "but I've put a log across the trail going up to the ledge. I don't want you going up there until this rain stops and things dry up a bit. I don't want you up there if there's a slide."

"There won't be a slide," said Natasha unconcernedly. "The root system there is quite extensive. It will hold the earth in place."

"No guarantee of that. So no going up there. I didn't put the log there because I don't trust you, I put it there to remind you," said Al.

"Because we all know what you're like, Miss Dozy," said Marlin.

"Marlin, you've had another rejection," said Al, taking second helpings of everything.

"OH, NO!" cried Marlin.

"Well, chin up. The book is still going out and if it makes you feel better, Steve is sending out my novel now too so I'll get my fair share of rejections and can commiserate with you."

"You'll probably get published right off the bat and I will go hang myself," said Marlin.

"Don't hang yourself," said Al. "Who will make me cake?"

"Mrs. Weatherspoon," said Fiona. "Or she would have before she joined Jo's anti-almost-all-foods club."

"Jo has her brainwashed," said Marlin.

"What's that?" asked Charlie.

"It's total mind control," said Marlin. "But we're going to rescue her and bring her back to the side of light and reason."

"Jo said she can make cakes," said Charlie. "She said you can make lots of things with dates instead of sugar and almond flour instead of wheat flour. She said they don't rise much but they're good for you."

"If they don't rise they aren't cakes. They're mud pies. Feh," said Marlin.

"What's it like these days with Georgia and the mean girls?" asked Al.

"Well, when I came in dressed head to toe in Gap, they were my friends, sort of. At least at first. Now they are mostly awful again but I am trying to get the mean girls to see just how hateful Georgia is. Although so far it isn't working. And worse, even though we finished our play, now Mrs. Dennison wants us all to stay in our same groups and work on a holiday-themed play as our English project. Of course, they want to do something stupid and easy like *The Elf Who Hated Toys*. That's actually their idea."

"That sounds good," said Charlie.

"No, it doesn't," said Marlin. "It's bad enough you're now Jo's little protégée, you can't be Georgia's too."

"I don't even know what that is," said Charlie.

"It's like an apprentice," said Fiona. "Sort of."

"Like her good little soldier," said Marlin bitterly.

"Where will Jo and Mrs. Weatherspoon sleep tonight?" asked Charlie.

"I assume they'll get a motel room like everyone else who can't make it through," said Al.

"They'll probably call as soon as they're settled. I'm surprised they didn't call from the road," said Marlin. "Jo is so addicted to her cell phone."

"Cell phones," said Al in disgust, and Fiona turned on the TV hurriedly because they'd all heard this rant dozens of times before. "The people who carry them pay no attention to the world around them, they think it's all in their phones. You see them walking around in Shoreline, teetering off sidewalks and tripping into cars and falling down open manholes because they're too busy on their phones."

"Falling down open manholes?" said Fiona, laughing.

"You have your computer," argued Marlin, who wanted a cell phone badly. "You stare at *that* electronic box all day."

"I use it for work. It's a tool. I stay off the internet and social media and all that nonsense and when my work is done, I close it."

"You get messages from Steve on it. You have iMessage and email," said Marlin.

"That's also for work, Marlin," said Al. "I'm not constantly on it playing games or talking to my friends."

"Well, anyway, Marlin, it's a moot point," said Fiona. "We can't afford to replace the cell phone or get a cell plan and we get no cell service out here anyhow."

"You hypocrite," said Marlin. "You told me the other night that half the kids at school your age have cell phones and you want one too. That everyone spends lunch hour texting everyone else. And we may not have cell service to call out but we can call the landline here when we'll be late if we have a cell."

"They can't afford the Gap but they all have cell phones?" said Al. "Has everyone gone mad?"

Then the phone rang. It was Mrs. Weatherspoon letting them know they had been turned around on the road home because of the slide and were driving back to Shoreline to find a motel. After that, everyone settled happily onto the couch for three games of *Jeopardy!* and another piece of cake.

—————

For two days the girls enjoyed having the house back to themselves and then the slide was cleared and Mrs. Weatherspoon and Jo returned beaming.

"Girls, girls, we have wonderful news!" said Mrs. Weatherspoon as the girls got home from school and all but Charlie sighed resignedly to find the pair once more on their doorstep. "We've done it! The mudslide turned out to be heaven-sent because we ended up being invited to stay with one of the new church members! Such a nice woman, Carol Simmons. And she invited over some friends and we had a wonderful evening and told them all about the church and the next night we had a potluck and—"

"And the upshot is that we have our *twenty* members. We can start an actual church and the Mother Church will send us a pastor when they find one and funds to rent a hall," said Jo. "Of course new members are a *pain,* if you want to know the truth, because they know *nothing* and you have to keep *explaining.* That's why I never wanted to do more than the office work in recruiting. And my feet are *killing me* after knocking on doors, not that that part is even *finished* yet."

"But we can really get going now. I think with any luck we'll have a church up and running and a pastor found by June!" said Mrs. Weatherspoon. "Oh, how I love meeting a goal."

"By *June*?" said Marlin. "You mean, I mean... you don't mean you plan to stay here until *June*? I thought you wanted to travel... to see Canada?"

"Oh, we'd have to stay to settle the pastor in," said Mrs. Weatherspoon. "We can start services without one but it would be terrible not to be here to welcome him or her. And to be practical, dear, as much as we'd love to see Canada by train, after looking into it in more detail, I doubt we can afford to see much. It's terribly expensive."

"Of course, I could have afforded it if I hadn't flown *all the way* to Australia only to fly *all the way* here," said Jo. "No, train travel turns out to be *crazy expensive*. So I guess staying here will have to be my *vacation*."

"So we may as well stay and make sure the church is all tickety-boo!" chimed in Mrs. Weatherspoon. "I must feel that we came here and did something useful before leaving. That is my goal."

"Oh, now, Mrs. Weatherspoon," said Marlin. "You mustn't think that way. That is, you *have* been useful. I can't tell you how useful. If there's a word for you, it's useful. And I think if you left, say, tomorrow, you can rest assured that we'd all say of you how useful you'd really been. Of much use. REALLY!"

"But Jo says we must stay until June, possibly next fall," said Mrs. Weatherspoon. "And I think you'll agree, she's very wise when it comes to these things."

"NEXT FALL?" squawked Marlin.

"Well, dear, I thought you would be happy," said Mrs. Weatherspoon.

"Mrs. Weatherspoon," said Fiona frantically, "I wonder if you could help me. I have a blouse with a spot I can't get out."

"Salt for stains, dear, what have I always told you, salt for stains."

"Yes, but, let me just show you."

Fiona led Mrs. Weatherspoon up to her bedroom. She dug in her laundry bag, for she did actually have a blouse with a troublesome stain. Then as she showed it to Mrs. Weatherspoon she said, "You know, do you find that Jo tends to say things about people behind their back?"

"What do you mean?" asked Mrs. Weatherspoon.

"Well, you know, she called Charlie hyperactive and Natasha weird and Marlin said she said you were taking too much medi—" Fiona stopped midword because although she desperately wanted to convince Mrs. Weatherspoon that Jo was bad news and hoped that if she did, Mrs. Weatherspoon would somehow detach herself and maybe even get rid of Jo herself, she could see it was not having the effect she wished for. Mrs. Weatherspoon had stopped studying the stain and was looking at Fiona askance.

"*You* seem to be the one saying things behind *Jo's* back!" said Mrs. Weatherspoon.

"Well, I know it appears that way," said Fiona, laughing in a self-deprecating way, "but I am only telling you this because I don't think Jo really always has the best intentions…"

"Are you sure *you* do, dear?" asked Mrs. Weatherspoon coldly.

Fiona, frustrated, thought, *Oh, Mrs. Weatherspoon, what has happened to you? She's got you.* At the same time, she knew Mrs. Weatherspoon had a point. She didn't sound as if she had the best intentions either. In fact, something she had been puzzling out for a while was how being around Jo, trying to defend against Jo, was somehow turning her *into* Jo. This might be the most destructive aspect of Jo and Fiona felt she had little control over it. Would they all be Jo by the time Jo left? She didn't know what to say to Mrs. Weatherspoon after that. So she said, "So do you think the stain will come out?"

"Salt for stains, dear, salt for stains," said Mrs. Weatherspoon in clipped tones, and put the blouse back in the laundry hamper and went back downstairs.

Fiona sat on her bed a little shocked. Now Mrs. Weatherspoon thought Fiona was the villain. And she was *never* the villain.

Marlin crept into the room after Mrs. Weatherspoon left.

"So?" she asked.

"Mrs. Weatherspoon thought I was trashing Jo," said Fiona.

"Well, weren't you?"

"I just wanted to plant a seed. Maybe I did. Maybe Mrs. Weatherspoon will think about it and see that I was right. Maybe it will put Jo in a different light. And if she sees who Jo really is then she can't be her good friend. She will see how evil and self-centered she is. Maybe she will even suggest she leave."

"Ha, that's a likely story," said Marlin. "Listen, Fiona, first of all, no matter what they say, they are *not* staying until next fall! And secondly, Fiona, I know it sounds awful—I mean I know it's not what Mom and Dad would want—but if they start a branch of the church the way they say they are, well, I'm not going. I understand if you and Charlie and Natasha want to, but I'm not."

"I don't want to go either," said Fiona. "And I don't think it sounds awful. I mean, Mom used to always tell me that when we were old enough she wanted us to make up our own minds about whether the church was right for us or not. But what about Natasha and Charlie? They aren't at that age yet. I know Mom would want them to keep going until they were old enough to make up their own minds."

"Well, but that's the thing. Mom and Dad *aren't* here. And we've had to do for ourselves. I think that gives us the right to make our own decisions and to make them for Charlie and Natasha too. Because we've had to be responsible for them whether we liked it or not. And if none of us are going to the church then Mrs. Weatherspoon and Jo don't have to stay on either because they keep saying they are starting it for us. If we don't want it then maybe there's no point to starting it."

"Oh, I doubt that would make a difference. They just like starting up new branches. We're just the excuse to start one here. I agree that we should find a way to make them leave," said Fiona. "I just don't know how."

"Well, figure it out," said Marlin. "I'll try to think of a way too."

Fiona nodded but she was still hesitant. Something about Jo waltzing off with Mrs. Weatherspoon blindly in tow wasn't sitting well with her. It felt too much like Jo winning. The mere thought enraged her. She didn't want them to stay but before they left she wanted to wrench Mrs. Weatherspoon out of Jo's clutches, if for no other reason than to spite Jo. And she really wanted Jo to see herself as Fiona saw her, horrible and selfish. That, if she was honest with herself, was what she wanted the most.

"I need to think some more," said Fiona. "Just give me time."

<hr />

Marlin gave Fiona time but November dripped on, rainy drizzly days, gray-sky days, and very little changed. Except that Georgia found a new way to torment Marlin.

"You know," she said to Marlin one day, sauntering over to Marlin's lonely lunch table, where no one sat with her despite her Gap Girl status. "I don't know why you think anyone will think it's special that a twelve-year-old can cook. Maybe you don't get the Food Network on TV."

"What do you mean?" asked Marlin patiently.

"Well, they have all kinds of kids' cooking competitions. There's the Kids' Food Championship. The Kids' Bake-Off. There are kids younger than you cooking. No one is going to think there's anything special about you cooking and making a cookbook. It's been done. And all those kids on TV are famous already. No one has ever heard of you. So why would they care about your book?"

Marlin had never heard of the Food Network or any of these kids' cooking and baking shows. A slow panic began to form. The question *Why would they care about your book?* went round and round her head.

"Well," she said loftily, "I guess if that were true, if no one would be likely to care, then I guess my agent wouldn't be bothering trying to sell my book."

"Yeah, *trying,* or so you say," said Georgia, and she smiled smugly and sauntered off.

Marlin had learned to mostly ignore the mean things Georgia said and did, but this one worried her. If Georgia was right, then Marlin's book was not such a novelty. She had counted on the novelty of a twelve-year-old being a good cook and baker to sell the book. She would write Steve about it when she got home. But that was another thing. For a while she had been writing Steve daily emails to check on whether there had been offers for her book. And Steve had grown tired of this. He told Al that if

Marlin wanted to be represented, from now on he would only communicate with her through Al. He hoped to stem the flood of daily emails this way and he did, because Al refused to write daily on her behalf.

"It's not professional, Marlin, it's just nagging," said Al. "You're going to blow it if you keep it up. No one wants to represent a nag."

She hadn't written Steve in a week but this was important. She would make Al flip him her letter. And then she would have perhaps a concrete professional opinion on the matter that she could use in defense the next time Georgia brought it up, which she no doubt would do daily now if she had caught on to how much she had upset Marlin with it.

Charlie alone of all the girls seemed as happy-go-lucky as always until the day Jo found a way to squelch this as well.

That day the girls came home from school and Jo met them saying, "Ashley's mother phoned." She then adopted a theatrically sympathetic look, pursing her lips and sitting down as if awaiting questions for which she had only very sad answers.

"Why?" asked Charlie.

"She got a call from their *BREEDER*," said Jo, stringing out the news in obvious pleasure at her own importance as the bearer of bad tidings. "The mama dog got pregnant."

Everyone cheered.

"Did the dog have puppies?" asked Charlie, who had no real sense of how long this took.

"No, that's just the thing," said Jo.

WHAT'S THE THING? FOR GOD'S SAKE SPIT IT OUT, Fiona wanted to yell, but Mrs. Weatherspoon was in the background watching this conversation and, Fiona thought, no doubt looking for signs of who was horrible, Fiona or Jo. Instead Fiona said, "Perhaps you'd better tell us what happened."

"The *DOG,* and I've never heard of this before so I really have to *WONDER* about that *BREEDER,* the *DOG* lost *all* the puppies."

"How could she lose them if they weren't born yet?" asked Charlie, looking mystified.

"She means the puppies died, Charlie," said Fiona. "There was a problem and the dog miscarried. Is that right, Jo?"

"Yes, and *the breeder* says it will be *months* before they try again."

"Months?" said Charlie. "But I wanted puppies for Christmas."

"Life is disappointing," said Jo. "Isn't it, Little Angel?"

"Well, now we can just explore different breeds," Marlin chimed in. "We aren't stuck with smooth collies now.

In fact, we could just go to the SPCA and adopt a couple of dogs and get this over with."

"No, that's just what you can't do. Now, girls, I've called pounds all over the island and no one has any dogs, much less puppies. They said there's a real shortage. And I was told there aren't even any breeders with puppies coming up that anyone knows of either."

"How can that be?" asked Marlin.

"Where are we going to get my puppies then?" said Charlie, beginning to cry.

"Now, Little Angel, I've had a much better idea," said Jo.

"What?" asked Marlin suspiciously.

"Cats," said Jo.

"We don't want cats," said Marlin, setting her face in what Fiona called her Mount Rushmore expression.

"Have you ever had cats?" asked Jo.

"No, I've never had lice either but I know I don't want them," said Marlin.

"Marlin," said Fiona.

"I think cats are a *LOVELY* idea," said Jo. "I really don't like dogs. Before, I thought, well, let the girls have their dirty little puppies since we'll be gone by January anyhow and won't have to *LIVE* with them but now that we're here until *JUNE, AT LEAST,* I think some nice clean cats are a better solution all around."

Marlin's face was a study in panic. Fiona almost laughed.

"Thanks, Jo," said Fiona. "But we're not getting cats. None of us like them or want them. We're getting dogs."

"And we're not going to church either," Marlin blurted out.

There was a stunned silence.

They were saved by the phone ringing. Fiona went into the office to pick it up so she didn't hear the discussion that had started up again in the living room.

On the other end of the line it was the elementary school's secretary wanting to set up a meeting with Natasha and Al for the following day with Natasha's music teacher, Mrs. Meyer.

"Why?" asked Fiona, thinking, *What now?*

"I don't know, dear," said Ms. Benedict, the secretary.

"Well, can you tell me if it's something bad?" asked Fiona.

"I can't imagine it is, can you? I've heard talk that your sister is quite the musician so I imagine it's good whatever it is. Perhaps it's something to do with the school concert."

"Do you think I could go then instead of Al?" asked Fiona. "I mean he would go if he had to but I know he has a magazine deadline."

"I can ask Mrs. Meyer for you, if you like," said Ms. Benedict.

"Thanks," said Fiona.

"I'll try and find Mrs. Meyer and let you know. Oh,

and by the way, Mrs. Meyer wants Natasha to bring her violin."

"To the meeting?" asked Fiona.

"Yes."

By the time they were done, the discussion in the living room had broken up but Mrs. Weatherspoon caught Fiona on her way upstairs by putting a hand on her shoulder and said, "My dear, what is this about you not going to the new church?"

"Oh, right," said Fiona, pausing for time to think, but she could find nothing that would work but the truth. "Well, we, that is Marlin and I, were discussing it and we decided we are old enough to make these decisions and well, I'm sorry, Mrs. Weatherspoon, but we don't want to go. It's nothing against the church, it's just that we've grown apart." She liked this way of putting it. She'd heard of friends' parents who were divorcing explaining it this way.

"Nonsense," said Mrs. Weatherspoon robustly. "Of course you're going and I don't want to hear another word about it. Your parents would never forgive me if they knew I let you drop out of the church."

Fiona was startled by Mrs. Weatherspoon's vehemence. Fiona was so flustered that she just nodded and continued upstairs without argument. She would think of how to deal with this later.

She wanted to tell Natasha about the meeting her music teacher had requested but Natasha was locked in her bedroom with violin music playing. So Fiona went to her own bedroom instead, where she found Marlin looking daggers.

"Well, that went well. While you were busy chatting on the phone Mrs. Weatherspoon said that we *had* to go to the new church and Jo said we can't check out any more dog breeders until we've all done a thorough investigation into cats. How dare she? She's nothing to us. She can't tell us what to do."

"Yes, Mrs. Weatherspoon told me that too. At least the church part. Ignore them both. They'll leave in January and we'll do what we like after that."

"Well, you may hope they leave in January but it sounds as if *they* plan to leave in June or even next fall. If then. Who phoned?"

"Ms. Benedict. Natasha and I are staying after school tomorrow to talk to her music teacher."

"Wow. This is the McCready year to get in trouble."

"It doesn't sound like trouble. At least Ms. Benedict didn't think so. She thinks it's just something to do with the school concert so I'm going with Natasha to the meeting instead of Al. Unless Mrs. Meyer, her music teacher, tells Ms. Benedict Al has to be there."

"So how are you getting home afterward?"

"I'll call Al or Mrs. Weatherspoon when we're done and ask someone to pick us up."

"Don't tell Mrs. Weatherspoon about the meeting beforehand, that's my advice," said Marlin. "Or you might get Jo sticking her nose in it like she did at my school meeting."

"Good point," said Fiona.

But the next day when Fiona got to the school office she found Al chatting with Ms. Benedict as he and Natasha waited for Mrs. Meyer to arrive.

"How did you know?" asked Fiona in surprise.

"Sorry, Fiona, I know you didn't want to bother Mr. Farber but Mrs. Meyer wanted him here too," said Ms. Benedict.

And just as she said that Mrs. Meyer arrived with a big smile on her face.

Whew, thought Fiona, so nothing too terrible. But Natasha still looked nervous. She was carrying her violin case, looking at the ground, and she shifted her weight from foot to foot as if she had to pee.

"Well, shall we?" said Mrs. Meyer after she had greeted them, gesturing to the empty office next to the principal's where such meetings were usually conducted.

"First of all, Natasha, you probably know what this meeting is about?" said Mrs. Meyer.

Natasha nodded her head miserably.

"I'd say something but I think really you need to hear it for yourself. Natasha, could you take out your violin and play for Mr. Farber and Fiona?"

Natasha looked dubious and fumbled with the latch of the case as if she wanted to prolong the moment forever.

Al, watching her, suddenly spoke up. "Mrs. Meyer, maybe it would help if I told you that as far as I'm concerned strings is a completely voluntary activity. If Natasha isn't enjoying it or having trouble with it, I don't need to hear her play. She can quit anytime as far as I'm concerned. I've never been one of those people who believe in making children do things they don't want to do or practice if they don't want to. If she's fallen behind, that's up to her. If she's—"

Mrs. Meyer looked perplexed. "Mr. Farber," she interrupted, "you've misunderstood completely. Natasha says she never plays for any of you. That she doesn't like to play in front of you."

"That's true," said Fiona.

"So you really don't know what I'm talking about?"

"Well, I get the gist, I think," said Al.

"I don't think you do," said Mrs. Meyer. "Natasha, why don't you play the Bach?"

Natasha, who had her violin out by now, picked it up, adjusted the bow, and then let loose with such a torrent of notes that it frightened Fiona. It was like listening to your dog suddenly speaking Italian or watching the squirrels in your backyard erupt into ballet. You simply couldn't take it in fully enough to respond. Fiona, glancing at Al, could see he was having the same trouble.

When she was done, Natasha put her violin and bow carefully back in the case and sat down again.

"Well...wow," said Fiona.

"How did this happen?" asked Al. It was an idiotic question but it was what Fiona wanted to know too.

"Well, that's the thing," said Mrs. Meyer. "This kind of talent, and really, you can't even call it talent..."

"Idiot savant," said Fiona. "She's an idiot savant. I saw a show on someone who could play the piano like that."

"I'm not an idiot," said Natasha.

"No, of course not," said Fiona, and shut her mouth. She didn't know what else to say.

"No, Fiona, I don't think we say idiot but she is a kind of savant, I would guess. That is, she has a kind of talent that I frankly am not equipped to deal with. I've had talented students come through before. Students who worked ahead in the music books and whose talent I could help to foster. But I've never had anyone chew up the books the way Natasha has. I couldn't ask you to keep buying her workbooks, she was going through them so quickly and it would be so expensive, so I've been giving her my old ones just to keep her busy. Hoping to challenge her. But nothing challenges her. I wanted you to hear, Mr. Farber, because it's kind of hard to believe until you do. And there are music schools for children this talented. I'm sure Natasha could easily acquire a full scholarship to one. I just felt that even though it is such early days, you needed to be aware. I mean, she can play in the school strings group but it's a joke. It's the beginning of the year, we're still working on pieces like 'O Christmas Tree' for the school concert. Natasha is way past bored with us."

"I'm not bored," said Natasha in her quiet little voice.

"Music schools?" said Al. "You mean now, at her age?"

"Yes. As you can probably figure, the island just doesn't have anything. Vancouver is the closest but not the best. Toronto..."

"You mean like *BOARDING* schools?" said Fiona.

"Yes. Well, I took the liberty of getting some brochures and information. I know Natasha has told me she isn't interested, but I think you really need to look at them. Maybe you can think about it over the holidays. What she has is very rare and it needs special care. She could have a brilliant, brilliant career in front of her."

After that Mrs. Meyer stood up. Al and Fiona remained seated for a moment, still in shock, and then finally Natasha nudged Fiona and said, "Come on, we have to go."

Al and Fiona followed Natasha out to the car in a daze.

"Wow," said Al when they got to the car.

They got in the car and sat for a moment. Al seemed to

have forgotten how to start it but finally he shook himself and drove them silently until they were almost home and then Natasha said, "I don't want to go to boarding school."

"No," said Al. "But, wow, can you ever play that thing." He turned to Fiona. "How could none of you know?"

"I didn't want anyone to know," said Natasha.

"Why?" asked Al.

"I just didn't. I just wanted to see if I could get into the strings."

"What does that mean?" asked Fiona.

"I just could feel that if instead of playing *on* the strings, if I could play deeper into them…anyhow, it doesn't matter. I don't want to do it anymore. I quit."

"You can't quit," said Fiona. "You're a genius."

"I don't care. I don't want to do it anymore."

"Okay," said Al. "Let's go in and have dinner. We can talk about it later."

"I don't want to talk about it," said Natasha. "I *never* want to talk about it."

"So you just want to quit now that everyone knows? *Because* everyone knows? Don't you enjoy it? You must enjoy it if you play that well," said Fiona, whose head was swimming.

She and Al and Natasha had paused on the porch, not wanting to continue the discussion indoors with the others until they knew where they all were with this.

"I liked it and now I don't want to do it anymore," said Natasha.

"Not ever?" asked Fiona.

"No," said Natasha.

Al looked at her for a moment. "Okay," he said. "That's that. I'm hungry. Let's go in and eat."

When they got inside and Natasha had run upstairs to put her violin away, Fiona whispered to him in the vestibule, "Okay? Just like that? We aren't going to argue with her?"

Al shrugged. "I guess a person doesn't have to do something just because she's good at it."

"But why does she want to quit? Do you think it's because of the boarding school thing? Do you think it's because she doesn't like the attention of being better than? What?"

"Fiona," said Al, sounding more like his irritable old self, "I don't know and I don't care. As far as I'm concerned Natasha has made up her mind and she doesn't want to talk about it. Basta."

Natasha came down along with Charlie and Marlin, who had been asking her repeatedly what the meeting had been about but had been met with silence.

Al was so stymied by something so unexpected from one of the girls he thought he knew and how to cope with it as their guardian that he actually sat down and put Jo's nut loaf on the plate in front of him.

Jo set another place, pointedly saying, "I *hope* I made *enough*."

"Where were you three?" asked Mrs. Weatherspoon. "Marlin would only say you were with Al."

"Jo, this nut loaf is dynamite!" said Al, changing the subject effectively because Jo then launched into a long monologue that included her nut loaf recipe and the many other nut loaf recipes in her repertoire and their nutritional benefits as opposed to meatloaf and how when she brought nut loaves to church potlucks, she always converted a few die-hard meat-eaters. And this reminded Mrs. Weatherspoon to update the girls on the church progress. Jo then interrupted Mrs. Weatherspoon to proceed into another long monologue about churches she had helped to set up worldwide.

"Are you a religious man, Al?" she asked in syrupy tones. "Will you be taking these girls to church?"

Al replied, "Not I. If the girls want to go that is entirely their own affair. As far as I'm concerned no one in this house need do anything she doesn't like."

"Well, that's no way to raise children," said Jo.

"That's the way I do it," said Al, who had had all his worst fears about dinner conversation with the houseguests confirmed. He stood up abruptly, whistled tunelessly, and left for his trailer.

That night when Marlin and Fiona lay in bed and

looked at the Big Dipper Marlin said, "I could tell you didn't want to say anything in front of Jo, but what was the meeting with Mrs. Meyer all about? The school concert? Did Natasha not have her part ready or something?"

"No, Natasha is a genius," said Fiona.

"Ha, ha," said Marlin. "What was it really about?"

"I mean it, really. She played this complicated Bach piece. It was weird. You know how she's always buried deep in her head so you don't know what's there? Well, that's what's there, apparently."

"What?"

"Musical genius. All that music we thought she was listening to on YouTube was really her playing. She's so brilliant that Mrs. Meyer wants her to go to some fancy music boarding school in Toronto for child prodigies."

"Well, good luck with that, Mrs. Meyer. We can't afford that, can we?"

"She said Natasha could get a full scholarship easily."

Marlin groaned.

"I know," said Fiona. "That's what I was thinking too. Natasha is too young to go away. But thankfully she doesn't want to anyway."

"No, I'm not groaning about that," said Marlin.

"What then?"

"It's just…" Marlin turned so her back was to Fiona. "It's just that I thought I was the one with all the talent in the family and now it turns out I can't even get published. It's not me who is the young genius…it's Natasha. She's the one who is going to make a zillion dollars and save the family."

"Well, you needn't worry," said Fiona. "She quit."

"What do you mean?"

"Just that. She quit strings."

"Why?"

"I don't know. She was just suddenly done with it."

There was a silence and then Marlin said, "That's just like Natasha, that's quintessential Natasha, isn't it? By the time you find out she's a genius, she's over it."

Fiona started laughing, then Marlin joined in, then they were sitting up, bent over with hysterical laughter, beating their fists on the bed, tears running down their faces. Neither one, if asked, could have explained what was so funny but it was the kind of laughter that rolfs all thought out of you and flows through you like a waterfall, washing you emotionally clean. They would just start to calm down, the laughter would die down, and then they would catch each other's eye and start all over again.

"Hey!" came Charlie's voice from the next room. "What's going on in there?"

"Nothing, nothing," Fiona choked out. "Go to sleep."

"You woke us up!"

"Sorry," said Fiona, gasping between laughs. "Sorry, sorry."

But she and Marlin continued snorting with laughter into their pillows for yet a while.

Finally, Fiona quieted enough to ask, "Is that why you want to get published so badly? To make money to save the family? Because I think we're going to be fine now, Marlin."

"I don't know," said Marlin. "But it would be horrible to find out that I have all the drive and Natasha has all the talent."

Marlin Gives Up

November was almost at an end. Natasha had returned her violin despite Mrs. Meyer's many protests and Al had had to make his position clear to a very confused music teacher that he was fine with Natasha's choice. Fiona didn't worry about Natasha, who was now interested in origami and spent hours doing complicated paper folding. There were paper cranes hanging all over the house.

But Fiona was worried about Marlin. Fiona had read how to vet puppies to decide which one you wanted. The article explained that you held a puppy on its back. You wanted a puppy that would struggle with you awhile but eventually give up. A dog that immediately gives up is too submissive. A dog that will never give up is too dominant. Marlin, thought Fiona, had always been that dominant dog. If you put her on her back, she would never stop struggling. It was therefore worrying when lately Marlin appeared to have stopped struggling over anything. She no longer struggled with Jo over the kitchen and had simply stopped cooking. She didn't appear to be struggling over Georgia and the mean girls because if Fiona brought it up, she just said, it's five against one, what am I supposed to do? She seemed tired and lethargic most of the time. It was as if because the thing that gave her the most pleasure, the thing at her wellspring, cooking and writing about it, had been taken away, she had no purpose. She was like a balloon from which the air had been let out and she went her floppy, wrinkled way through her days.

Marlin could have told Fiona that this was only part of the problem. She found Jo unbearable and her own anger toward her exhausting, but she could have dealt with it had she not also had to deal with Georgia and the mean girls and the constant rejection slips from publishers too. Between those three things she felt she had no foothold within herself and without one she didn't exist as Marlin. She went through her days with no joy because the Marlin who felt joy didn't exist. No one, not Mrs. Dennison, who censored her, not Jo, who belittled her, not Georgia and the mean girls, who hated her, or the publishers, who couldn't seem to see what she had to offer, allowed for her existence.

Every day was a trial at school. Especially on Tuesday mornings when everyone rehearsed for the holiday concert. It was bad enough that Georgia had decided their play would be about an elf who hated toys. It was bad enough that Marlin was going to have to take part credit for a play she wasn't allowed to help write and which she found embarrassingly bad. A play that involved a stupid elf who bumbled about with comic intentions although not comically, through a number of scenes beginning with one where he was pinched by all the toys, then thrown into a snowdrift and left to freeze to death. But, to top it off, Marlin was ordered to take the part of the elf.

"I don't want to do it," she said hopelessly as they handed her the script.

"Why not? It's the main part. It's the lead. We're paying you a compliment by offering it to you," said Georgia.

"You just want me to be the elf because you want to pinch me and throw me into the arctic snows," said Marlin. "What kind of a holiday play is this, anyway?"

"It's a poignant social drama," said Georgia.

Marlin's jaw dropped that there would be such a cogent answer from someone who had been writing dialogue for the elf that went, "Here, Slinky, slink *THIS!*"

Naturally Marlin was unable to talk the girls into giving her a different part and naturally the girls wanted a full-on rehearsal every Tuesday so they could practice their pinching skills. Mrs. Dennison came over once when she said she noticed that their rehearsals seemed to be getting a little rough what with all the yipping noises coming from Marlin.

"Rest assured, Mrs. Dennison," said Georgia, "we

aren't really *hurting* Marlin. She's supposed to make those noises. It's scripted."

"Well, thank heavens for that," said Mrs. Dennison. "We don't want anyone getting hurt. Even Marlin."

Marlin's head snapped around and she stared at Mrs. Dennison in disbelief. Mrs. Dennison gave herself a little shake and said, "That didn't come out right. I didn't mean even *Marlin*. I meant, even...anyone!"

Marlin started to open her mouth and then closed it again. In keeping with her general attitude toward life these days, she didn't believe she could stem the tide of abuse. So why bother complaining? Also, she figured Mrs. Dennison had unwittingly revealed her real feelings. Even *Marlin*, indeed. Life was not worth living.

Marlin started to come home covered in bruises but when Mrs. Weatherspoon asked her why she was so black and blue she would only say, "The school play," and wouldn't elaborate. She told Fiona, of course, and Fiona worried more and more but didn't know what she could do about it if Marlin wouldn't let her and Marlin wouldn't. She said telling would only make things worse.

Meanwhile Charlie, ever the optimist, who had even bounced back from the puppy crisis, came home one day looking worried and said to Fiona, "Where are Mommy's and Daddy's trophies and medals? Did they did get washed away in the tsunami too?"

"What are you talking about?" asked Fiona. She knew Charlie had that whole horrible time mixed up and vague in her head. "You know Mommy and Daddy were on vacation in Thailand. Why would they have trophies and medals with them? What trophies and what medals and why do you need to know?"

"Because our teacher wants us all to bring into school things that our heroes have done," said Charlie. She handed Fiona the written notice about this.

"A hero table," read Fiona. She read the notice through and then said, "So you're making a hero table to display in the hallway in December. Everyone needs to bring in things representing their chosen hero. A trophy or medal if it's someone close to you, something that represents an achievement. Or a photograph if the hero is a public figure. Plus an inspirational saying that represents the values of the hero or which the hero is fond of. So Mommy and Daddy are your picks for the hero table?"

Charlie nodded solemnly and Fiona felt like crying. She blinked away tears and then said, "Right. Well, I'm not sure we have any old trophies or medals but I can look into it."

"What inspirational sayings are you using?" asked Marlin.

"Daddy always said 'Don't rain on anyone's parade,'" said Charlie.

"I don't think that's an inspirational saying—" began Marlin, but seeing Charlie's face, Fiona interrupted Marlin and said, "If that's what you remember Daddy saying then you should use that."

"But I don't know what Mommy's saying should be," said Charlie.

"I do," said Marlin. "She read it to me once. She said it was her favorite book passage and helped her whenever she read it. I'll look it up."

Marlin disappeared into the office, where they stored the few books they had brought with them. One was their mother's favorite. Marlin scanned the pages until she found the passage her mother had highlighted. She brought it in and said, "Here, Charlie, this is it. 'When you see a special light in someone else, it not only reaffirms that such light exists, but once more you find your own.' Shall I print that out for you?"

"It's kind of long, isn't it?" asked Fiona. "I mean, to be printed on a card for the hero table?"

"I don't know, I just know Mom said it was her favorite passage," said Marlin.

"I want it," said Charlie.

"Okay," said Fiona quickly. "Well, let me think about the trophies and medals then, Charlie. I'm sure they did something special but I just need time to remember."

Fiona wracked her brains after that. She knew there

were no medals or trophies or certificates. She would certainly have packed them when they came to Pine Island if there had been. She asked Mrs. Weatherspoon, who had known her parents, if she could remember anything special her parents had done and Jo chimed in to say, "You know we can't all be leaders. Some of us have to be sheep. There's nothing wrong with being an ordinary person with no special skills."

"I wouldn't say they were ordinary with no special skills," said Fiona, trying to keep her irritation in check.

"Oh?" said Jo, in the tone of someone anxious to be corrected. "What *were* their special contributions?"

Fiona thought. She wanted to yell, *It's none of your business,* but she bit her lower lip until she could say, "Well, Charlie's teacher is asking about trophies. I'm just concentrating on that right now."

"Oh, I see," said Jo smugly. "Well, you concentrate on *that* then."

Fiona looked over to Marlin to see if she was balling up her fists, sitting up, or getting ready for battle. Fiona always felt like the owner of a barking dog in such circumstances, ready to race forward, grab the lead, and quiet the dog, but Marlin just lay apathetically on the couch flipping TV channels and looking uninterested. This, thought Fiona, was far worse than Marlin barking. She would far rather have to try to calm Marlin down than rev her up.

"Anyhow, Charlie, don't worry," said Fiona. "We'll find something."

"Okay," said Charlie, cheering up and going upstairs to get her fashion dolls.

That night as they lay in their beds Fiona said to Marlin, "What are we going to do about this stupid hero table? I can't think of any medals or trophies Mom or Dad had. If they had them they didn't pack them and take them around the world. Do you think we could just make one up for Charlie? Maybe buy something in Shoreline that looks like a trophy?"

"Who cares anyway?" said Marlin. "Why doesn't she just tell the teacher that they didn't do anything special and then they died. That ought to shut up the teacher."

Fiona rolled over in shock and looked at Marlin. "How can you say that? Of course they did special things. They... they raised us."

"Bravo," said Marlin. "Have Charlie tell the teacher they got the parent trophy."

"What's the matter, Marlin?" asked Fiona, still in shocked tones.

"Nothing," said Marlin. "Everything is fine."

The next day Fiona wrote in her journal, *Why didn't we ask our parents more questions when they were alive? I know practically nothing about them as people now. I don't know if they got trophies and medals or certificates when* they were younger. I hardly know anything about them at all. I mean I know them as our parents but not as people who had lives outside us at one point. And now Charlie won't either. And she has to go to school with nothing not only to show other people but if they did do special things, she will never know.

To this Mr. Byrne wrote, *How could she have lived with them and not have the things she knew about them be really the most important things to know? What could a trophy tell her that they hadn't already told her by the way they lived their lives? That's what I found when my mother died. What she left behind for me was that memory of her life, the part I had lived with her. She had trophies but who cared? It's the loss of the person that we grieve, not their achievements. That's one of the reasons my father moved to Vancouver, I think. To get away from his grief.*

But you can't, can you? wrote Fiona.

You don't even really want to, do you? he wrote back.

You do, she said, *but you don't.*

Yes, Fiona, he wrote, *you do, but you don't.*

She wrote back, *What I want to find out, what I really want to find out is how it all works. I mean when you die. Do you die and then you are but aren't conscious and you remain that way until you come into consciousness again when you become something else or has it all been a great colossal waste of time because everything you discover and*

*learn and experience just gets lost when you die so that
even if you do reincarnate or something, you are just starting from scratch and all the love you have ever felt for the
people you really love is just lost too. Isn't that unbearable?
Not that our bodies are gone but that our love is. But if it
isn't, what happens with all of it? What happens at all? I
think about it—all of this—all the time. It haunts me. How
does it work? How does it happen? And we none of us ever
know. We can wonder all we like and when we do die we
may find out but we may not know we find out because we
are already gone. Or we may never find out that there never
was anything to find out.*

Do you think you wonder about this so obsessively
because *your parents died?* asked Mr. Byrne.

No, wrote Fiona, *I worried about it all the time before
that. Didn't you?*

Yes, wrote Mr. Byrne. *All the time. Sometimes I think all
worries are really about this, only disguised as other things.*

Fiona realized she had never voiced these thoughts
to anyone, even in writing. She had never had a friend
to whom she could talk about these things. Mr. Byrne,
despite the difference in their ages, was a friend. Because to
whom but a dear friend could you confess such thoughts?
And what was a friend except a person who was so on
your wavelength that you felt safe telling your innermost
thoughts? Friends came in all genders and ages, thought

Fiona. But she and Mr. Byrne could not openly be friends. People would laugh at the idea of a fifteen-year-old girl and a forty-year-old man being intellectual equals. Yet they were. He was her superior in experience only. They were paired by what concerned them. What got their attention and what mattered to them. What they laughed at and what they didn't.

But something else was happening to Fiona with her honest and more in-depth journal entries. She was learning what she thought by writing, just as Mr. Byrne had told the class they would. And in doing so she was becoming friends with herself.

When Fiona told Marlin what Mr. Byrne said, Marlin said, "Listen, that's all well and good but Charlie just wants to bring something in to put on the hero table with all the other trophies and stuff. We'd better find something."

So Fiona knocked on Al's trailer door, went in, and said, "Do you have anything that looks like an award or a trophy that I could give to Charlie and lie that it was won by our parents?"

Before he asked why, Al started rooting through his messy desk drawers and finally pulled out a medal and a miniature trophy.

"Here," he said. "I take it this is for school?"

"All the kids are supposed to bring some kind of trophy their hero won."

Al scoffed.

Fiona examined the medal and miniature trophy.

"I got the medal for track in high school but it doesn't have my name on it," he said. "And this was a joke from your great-aunt."

The trophy said FRESNO BOWLING CHAMPION.

"What does it mean?" asked Fiona. "Why did she give it to you?"

"Never mind, private joke and I'd like it back when Charlie is done with it," said Al.

"How do we explain that to Charlie?" asked Fiona. "She will probably want to display them in the house when she brings them home again from school."

"Never mind," said Al, waving her away. "Sic transit gloria mundi. Just let her keep them."

Fiona put the medal and tiny trophy in her coat pocket and went back to the house.

Upstairs Marlin was lying on her bed doing homework. Fiona showed her the trophy and medal.

"Huh," said Marlin. "That should work."

"Marlin," said Fiona enticingly, "Mrs. Weatherspoon and Jo haven't come back yet from Shoreline. You could take this opportunity to make supper."

"And then spend the evening listening to Jo complain about it?" said Marlin.

"Well, we'd still get a good supper out of it," said Fiona.

"Why bother?"

Fiona frowned. She settled down to do her homework but she worried.

"Maybe, Marlin," she began, trying to find some way to infuse Marlin with her old fighting spirit, but at that second the girls heard the sound of the car pulling up in front of the house and a second later they heard Mrs. Weatherspoon calling, "Girls! Girls! Great excitement! Come down and see!"

"A new variety of lentil?" said Marlin dispiritedly, and kept writing out her math equations.

"Well, you might as well go down and see," said Fiona.

"Why bother?" said Marlin. This seemed to be her new mantra.

"Come on," Fiona urged, pulling at Marlin's sweater. So Marlin heaved a sigh and headed down the stairs. Charlie and Natasha were already there sitting on the couch, each of them holding a ginger kitten.

Marlin froze.

"What's this?" she asked. "I thought we said no cats."

"Yes, what *is* this?" asked Fiona.

"Well, girls, I know you said you wanted *DOGS*," said Jo. "But we couldn't pass up the opportunity, we really *couldn't*. The Simmonses, that's *that nice family* who invited us to stay after the *mudslide*, their cat had *KIT-TENS a few weeks ago* and Carol Simmons said we could have *two. IMAGINE!* Of course, you'll have to pay the *vet bills* and get them their *shots* and stuff but we already stopped at Walmart and picked up kitty litter and a litter box and some food."

"We can go back to Walmart for the rest," said Mrs. Weatherspoon. "We thought you'd like to pick out the cat toys and such yourselves."

"This one is *Mittens* and this one is *Puff,*" said Jo.

"Who named them?" asked Marlin.

"*I* did," said Jo. "They just *looked* like Mittens and Puff to me."

"But we wanted to name our pets," said Charlie.

"Now, Little Angel, *I* got the cats for you. The *least* you can do is let me *name* them," said Jo.

"We don't want cats, we want dogs," said Marlin with something resembling her old fighting spirit.

"I explained why you can't have dogs," said Jo curtly. "There *ARE* no dogs. And, well, you've got cats. Now, I'd better start dinner."

"I think you hurt her feelings, girls," whispered Mrs. Weatherspoon when Jo had gone into the kitchen. "She thought you'd be so excited."

"Why?" whispered Fiona. "We told her we wanted dogs."

"Look how happy the little girls are," said Mrs. Weatherspoon. "Now, you wouldn't want to separate those little girls from their new kittens, would you?"

Marlin stomped upstairs and refused to come down-stairs to eat. She stomped downstairs again to get a box of crackers and then returned to her room, slamming the door. She refused to speak to anyone the rest of the evening. Fiona tried to remain upbeat and keep things normal for the little girls during dinner but Charlie kept asking what was wrong with Marlin and there was a strained atmosphere in the house. Jo said Charlie was squeezing Puff too hard and perhaps she was too young to pick up kittens. Natasha immediately dropped hers and went to her room as if afraid Jo would admonish her too. Charlie cried. Mrs. Weatherspoon tried to comfort her and Jo said, "Well, being a *crybaby* solves *nothing*. I have a thought to *cheer you up, very soon* is the first service in our new *meeting hall.* All you girls will come, of course. Do you have appropriate clothes?"

"I'm not a crybaby," said Charlie.

"No, of course you're not, Little Angel. Shall we go through your closet and see what you can wear to church?"

"I want to wear my fashion doll dress that I got for Halloween," said Charlie.

Fiona couldn't bring herself to remind them that nei-ther she nor Marlin planned to go to the new church. Instead she was having second thoughts about skipping it. To skip it would be to give Natasha and Charlie to Jo and her bad influence. Fiona was unwilling to do this even for one morning a week. Fiona wanted to discuss it with Marlin but Marlin was in no mood for such discussion. Meanwhile Mittens knocked over a glass and shattered glass became the more pressing issue. By the time Fiona went to bed she was exhausted.

The next day at school Fiona was preoccupied with Mr. Byrne. She had used the word febrile wrong in her journal and he began the day by teasingly inserting it into whatever he was saying in class at every opportunity without looking at her. She started to laugh and the more it happened, the funnier it became, made more so by the fact that no one else knew what was going on.

Toward the end of the day a guest speaker came to talk about the junior chamber of commerce in Shoreline. He was a dull man and he made corny jokes as part of his patter. It made Fiona wince although she kept a polite face. Mr. Byrne amused himself by passing her silly notes quietly with a serious face throughout the speaker's lecture.

Febrile—a very long guest lecture, he wrote.

She wrote back beneath this and politely passed it back to him. *Febrile—the pathetic attempt to make jokes only slightly funnier than the speaker's.*

Mr. Byrne wrote beneath: *Febrile—someone whose comments are often hilarious and accurate but she is too cowardly to share them with the class. I bet you don't raise your hand when he asks for questions.*

Beneath this comment she replied: *Arrogant—someone who thinks I must be more interested in his notes than listening to the speaker.*

Fiona worried she had gone too far this time but Mr. Byrne read this one and smiled.

Later that night Fiona wrote in her journal, *Mr. Byrne gives me hope that life after high school will come with more interesting, more simpatico friendships than those I have had up until now. That adulthood will be a more interesting time in general.* Then she ripped this page out of the book. She realized that her journal entries were becoming more truthful but that she didn't want to share everything she was discovering with Mr. Byrne. That her journal was no longer just a school assignment or a way to show off how smart she was to someone who seemed to appreciate it, but an important but private conversation with herself. She felt really she should be keeping two journals now. The one she shared and the one that was just for her.

December

As December started, the girls began to get excited about Christmas. They had been too grief-stricken the year before to celebrate it. Marlin and Fiona went into the attic hoping to find some Christmas decorations but Aunt Martha had none so the girls decided to make what they could. They made wreaths easily enough with all the fallen pine boughs on the ground and there was plenty of waxy green holly with bright red berries, which grew wild all over the island, as well as red arbutus tree berries on thin branches and rose hips left over from summer. The house soon became festively green and red. Al had promised to take them in the truck to buy a tree at St. Mary's Church in St. Mary's By the Sea, where they were sold as a fundraiser.

"We can buy a couple of boxes of glass ornaments at Walmart," said Fiona as the girls buzzed about getting ready for school one morning. "And for the rest, we can string popcorn and cranberries and make paper chains."

"I can bake some homemade Play-Doh ornaments

with holes to string ribbon through and we can all paint them," contributed Marlin.

"What about presents?" asked Charlie. "Ashley still believes in Santa Claus."

The girls' parents had never encouraged a belief in Santa, feeling it was akin to lying to them. Marlin had always wondered how anyone was silly enough to actually believe in some fat man coming down the chimney anyway.

"Oh, Santa exists, Little Angel," said Jo, who was listening in.

"No, he doesn't," said Charlie. "Mommy and Daddy already told me they brought presents, not Santa."

"Oh, but he does," insisted Jo. "And you *must* believe in him or you won't get a *Santa* of your own magically appearing in your pocket."

"What pocket?" asked Charlie, feeling her pajama pants. "I don't have a pocket."

"You'll see," said Jo, and began the tuneless humming she did that always set Marlin's teeth on edge.

The other girls thought this was just more of Jo's silliness and making herself important and were too busy running about getting ready for school to pay it much attention.

But as they stood at the end of their driveway waiting for the bus, Natasha felt her jacket pocket, pulled out a Santa pencil topper, and said, "Where did this come from?"

The other girls stared at it in surprise. Since Jo had just mentioned Santas they knew it must be from her but Jo had always been more of a taker than a giver so it surprised them and they began madly feeling their own pockets.

Marlin and Fiona pulled out their own Santa pencil toppers but Charlie felt around frantically in all her pockets and couldn't find one. "Maybe it's in my backpack," she said hopefully, taking it off and beginning to rifle through it, but just then the bus came and Fiona helped her scoop it up and the girls leapt onto the bus.

As they rode, Charlie continued to look. "I didn't get one," she said finally.

"Oh, that Jo," said Marlin in disgust. "It's because you said you didn't believe in Santa."

Charlie's face melted and she began to cry.

"Here," said Fiona, quickly giving Charlie her Santa. "Have mine."

"Mommy and Daddy said there wasn't any Santa," Charlie cried.

"And there isn't," said Marlin. "Jo is insane."

"Hush," said Fiona. "Charlie, don't worry about it. I'm sure she just forgot yours."

"Right," said Marlin sarcastically.

"Hush," said Fiona. "Let's all try to have a good day."

"I never have a good day," said Marlin.

"Marlin," said Fiona. "How can you say that?"

"I'm just speaking truth the way Charlie did. Is no one in this family allowed to tell the truth?" Marlin dragged herself wearily off the bus and into school with Fiona staring worriedly after her.

The morning for Marlin began well enough but when they began their rehearsals for *The Elf Who Hated Toys*, she found that overnight Georgia and the mean girls had been talking to each other on the phone and had rewritten the script.

"It's a few minor changes," Georgia said to Marlin patronizingly. "Nothing too drastic. No lines of *yours* changed so we didn't make an extra copy of the new script for you."

"Fine," said Marlin, thinking, *I couldn't care less.*

The play began as usual but when they got to the scene where the elf declares she doesn't like toys the doll's first new line was "Wait a second, what was that I heard? Did the elf just *FART*?"

Marlin stopped. "I won't do it," she declared.

"What do you mean?" said Georgia.

"You take that out or I won't do the play."

"You'll get a big fat zero on your report card. Mrs. Dennison will *make* you do it," said one of the mean girls.

"Now, Marlin," said Georgia in her most syrupy manner, "this is a great twist. It's going to be *so FUNNY*. And you'll get the biggest laugh."

"Forget it. Listen, how stupid do you think I am? People will be laughing *at* me, not with me," said Marlin.

"Not stupid…" said one mean girl.

"A little flatulent maybe…" giggled a second.

Then all the girls giggled.

"No," said Marlin.

"Oh, come on, be a sport," said another mean girl.

"No, I'm tired of being a sport," said Marlin. "I'm not doing it. And I'll tell Mrs. Dennison why. Or I'll tell some older boys I know and they'll…"

"What?" said one of the mean girls. "Beat us up?"

"Well, you'll have to wait and find out, won't you?" spat out Marlin, but her spirits sank even further. She had reached rock bottom with this empty threat. She knew no older boys. And what had happened to her, hinting at violence? She was both furious and afraid of what she would do next. She wasn't just becoming a mean girl herself, she was becoming *worse* than the mean girls.

"If you tell Mrs. Dennison you'll get the reputation all over school for being a tattletale and no one will want anything to do with you EVER AGAIN," said Georgia.

The rest of rehearsal went according to the new script except that Marlin sat stonily in her chair, refusing to act or say her lines. She felt so stuck. If she did nothing, the mean girls would roll right over her. If she defended herself she felt equally horrible, mean and small and weaker than if she did nothing. She had no idea how to be around people like Jo and Georgia and the mean girls. She was full of impotent rage.

The girls didn't seem to mind that Marlin sat silently and Georgia even seemed exultant that Marlin was so upset. Marlin realized miserably that she had given Georgia exactly the reaction she had wanted. The girls ran through the play over and over as if Marlin were participating. And the rest of the morning after that was spent with Georgia and the mean girls passing notes to each other, looking at Marlin and giggling.

At lunch Marlin sat alone at her table and tried to pretend she wasn't completely destroyed, lonely, upset, angry, and impotent. She stared ahead, hardly able to eat. She knew that if she tattled she would be done for, that much she knew to be true, but equally if she didn't, if she put up with the fart joke, she would be humiliated. She was contemplating the idea of a boarding school in Shoreline again when to her amazement Jeannie Eisenberg, a girl from her class whom she'd never actually spoken to, came and sat down across from her. Marlin was so surprised she just stared stupidly and somewhat rudely at her.

"Hi," said Jeannie, who looked like a small gray mouse and sounded like one too.

"Hi," replied Marlin warily.

"You were new last year."

"Yes?" said Marlin. She was so used to being tormented that she trusted no one, even though Jeannie had a kind, happy face atop her tiny body.

"I'm in a group with five boys. For the plays? Mrs. Dennison made them take me because I couldn't find another group. I avoid those girls you got stuck with. I saw Mrs. Dennison lead you over to them and I thought, *Uh-oh*."

"Uh-oh is right," said Marlin.

"I guess that means you're not happy to be with them."

"I guess we're both unhappy in our groups," said Marlin. "What do you suggest?"

"How about you change groups?" said Jeannie.

"Mrs. Dennison said that if I switched groups everyone would wonder why," said Marlin.

"Why would anyone care?" asked Jeannie. "I want another girl in my group. Other than that, I'm not really unhappy with it. If you joined us, then Ted could go into *your* group. He hates ours. The other boys pick on him because he's short."

Marlin said nothing but she was thinking Jeannie was even shorter.

"They don't mind it in a girl," said Jeannie as if reading her mind.

"As if there's anything wrong with that anyway," said Marlin.

"Yeah," Jeannie agreed matter-of-factly. "Well, so, I asked him, I said, maybe he could switch groups with *you*. He'd be with a bunch of girls but at least he wouldn't be picked on. He said yes."

"He might still get picked on. Listen, full disclosure, I doubt he will want to play the elf who gets pinched and farts."

"I bet they'll stop pinching when he has the part," said Jeannie. "I bet they only want to pinch *you*."

Marlin was surprised at Jeannie's quick and accurate assessment and also that although this was a solution that would solve everything for her, she felt oddly hesitant to leave Georgia and the mean girls. She was reluctant to admit that it felt as if Georgia and the mean girls hadn't wanted her and so would win. And she was no closer than before to knowing how to deal with such girls. But to say these things would sound petty. Instead she said, "Well, I think your fix is kind of genius."

"Oh, no," said Jeannie, looking down at the table with pink cheeks. "I'm just a B student really."

"Well, I think it's a genius solution, but the question is will Mrs. Dennison go for it?" said Marlin.

"Let's go ask her. She eats lunch in the classroom." Jeannie started to stand up.

"Here," said Marlin, suddenly so flooded with gratitude that she gave Jeannie her Santa pencil topper.

Jeannie looked surprised. "Wow, thanks. Are you sure?"

Marlin nodded.

"Okay, come on." Jeannie grabbed her things and Marlin barely had time to pack up her lunch remains before racing after Jeannie, who was striding purposefully back to the classroom on her short legs.

Mrs. Dennison was alone in the classroom finishing a tuna sandwich when the girls arrived breathless. She seemed surprised by the request.

"Does Ted know about this?" she asked.

"Oh, it was his idea," said Jeannie.

"What about all the other kids in the two groups? Will they be all right with this sudden change?"

"Everyone will be happy," lied Marlin. She had no idea if anyone would be happy except for her and Jeannie and Ted. She suspected not but she really didn't care.

"Well, all right," said Mrs. Dennison. "I'm sure there's plenty of time left for you and Ted to learn your new parts. And we do want happy holiday plays. I was thinking they could be performed at the big holiday concert."

"The elementary and the secondary school have a joint holiday concert every year," Jeannie explained to Marlin.

Thank God I am switching groups, thought Marlin. The idea of her family and of Al and Mrs. Weatherspoon and, worst of all, Jo, coming to watch her fart and be pinched made her blood run cold.

Later, when everyone came back from lunch, Mrs. Dennison took Jeannie, Marlin, and Ted with her to talk to the two groups involved. Georgia's face was a study. She looked like a cat who had had a particularly toothsome baby bird taken from her.

"I think Marlin should remain in her part as the elf," she said.

"Why?" asked Mrs. Dennison, a flicker of light in her eyes.

"Because…because she needs to finish what she starts," said Georgia.

"Oh, Georgia, don't be ridiculous!" snapped Mrs. Dennison. "Ted and Marlin are going to change parts and everyone is going to get along with their new cast members and I don't want to hear any more about it."

Saved, thought Marlin. *Saved.* And by the mousiest, quietest girl in the school, the last person she would have thought would have swooped in and rescued her from what Georgia and the mean girls had almost convinced her was her just desserts. Because that had been the terrible thing, not that she had been so tormented but that because of their constant torment and so many of them and only one of her, she had begun to believe that at some level they might be right.

On the bus ride home, Fiona noticed Marlin's changed mood. But she was reluctant to ask what was up with her. Now that she was writing about everything in her journal, now that she had Mr. Byrne to talk to, she didn't confide so much in Marlin anymore, or at least confided different things to Marlin than she confided to her journal and Mr. Byrne. She felt that her friendship with Mr. Byrne was oddly disloyal to Marlin and never brought it up. It felt wrong asking for confidences when she was offering less than she used to in return herself. But, fortunately, Marlin had decided to relate the new turn of events of her own volition.

"That's fantastic," said Fiona when Marlin had finished. "So you have a friend."

"I think I do," said Marlin, looking surprised all over again.

"What's she like?"

"Well, she's not like me at all. She's really nice…" said Marlin, and realized what she'd said and laughed.

The bus let the girls off. Charlie and Natasha, who had sat at the front of the bus chattering away to each other, ran up the driveway ahead of Fiona and Marlin.

"I'm going to go knock on the trailer," said Fiona. "Al keeps promising to get the tree and the good ones will all be gone if we don't hurry. And I want him to take me into Walmart soon if he can. I'm going to do stockings for everyone."

"Oh, hooray!" said Marlin. "I didn't know you'd planned that."

"Well, I'm doing them for all of us but do you think I need to do them for the grown-ups? I mean, Mom and Dad never got one but in some families the parents get them. The girls I lunch with have been talking about their Christmases and Sarah says her parents always do a stocking for each other."

"No, I don't think we have to. Certainly not for Jo. Since we're splitting the grocery budget with them, we're already spending enough of our money on lentils. But what about presents?"

"I've got that covered. For everyone, not just the four of us. But I'm not telling you what. It's a surprise," said Fiona.

"Can I come into town with you and Al?"

"No," said Fiona. "I want to keep it as a surprise for you too."

Marlin skipped into the house. She planned to make Christmas cookies. She'd been too cowed to reclaim her kitchen during her period of defeat by the world, but now she had a friend and she felt reenergized and pitied Jo if she got in her way.

Fiona went to Al's trailer and knocked on the door. He flung it open, yelling as he often did when his work was interrupted, "WHAT?"

"I thought you had your book out the door," Fiona said in surprise because his hair was all ruffled on end and he had the wild look he bore when he was in a writing frenzy.

"Just because I'm no longer writing my book doesn't mean I'm not writing, Fiona. How do you think I pay for all this?"

"All what?" answered Fiona mildly. "We own the house and the land."

"What do you want?"

"I wondered when you'd have time to get the tree."

"Come on!" he said, grabbing his coat and his car keys and stomping down the steps with her in tow. "Hurry up. I can see I won't have a moment's peace until we have that stupid tree in your living room."

"We need a tree stand first," said Fiona. "I thought we could go to Walmart."

"Not today. No time. Hurry up, get in the truck."

"But what will we put the tree in?"

"We can get a tree stand at Drucker's Hardware. I've seen them there."

"It will cost a fortune," said Fiona worriedly. "You

know he charges twice or even three times what you'd pay at Walmart."

"Don't you want to support the local economy?" asked Al with an evil sparkle in his eye. Sometimes he and Marlin seemed much alike to Fiona.

"Not at double the price," said Fiona.

"Well, what do you think it costs in gas and time to *get* to Walmart?" asked Al. "Ever think of *that*?"

"I know, but I have a whole long list of things to get there," said Fiona as they sped toward St. Mary's By the Sea. "I want to make the girls stockings for Christmas. That's what we always used to have."

"And a lot of presents, I suppose?" said Al.

"No, we each got one present. That was the rule. One present but also a stocking. So I need to shop. I want what's in the stockings to be a surprise, of course. And I want to get some tree ornaments. A tree skirt. Stocking stuffers. I can't get all that at Drucker's."

"All right," said Al. "But I can't say when exactly I can take you to Walmart. I'm in the middle of two magazine pieces. Can't you get Mrs. Weatherspoon to do it?"

Fiona didn't want to voice her concern, which was that Mrs. Weatherspoon and Jo might agree to take her but she was worried that she would somehow end up being brought around and introduced to the new church members. Fiona didn't know why she was so afraid of this.

She knew it was irrational to believe that as long as she could avoid meeting these new church people she would escape being unwittingly sucked back into the giant maw of the church. But also, being with Jo and Mrs. Weatherspoon had become increasingly unpleasant as they grew closer, like two evil twins, with their judgments and harsh expressions. Fiona had begun to feel that all four sisters were constantly wanting in their eyes.

"I don't want to go with them," said Fiona. "Can't you take me, please?"

"All right. But you'll have to go when it's a good time for me," said Al.

"That's okay," said Fiona. "I can wait."

They drove quietly for a bit and then Fiona said, "Only not too long."

"Fiona…" said Al warningly, and then they pulled into the St. Mary's Church parking lot.

Fiona and Al examined all the trees for sale, finally selecting a large Douglas fir that had a wonderful thick piney scent. They picked up a stand and some lights from Drucker's with Fiona rolling her eyes at the prices. Then they drove home and Al spent a few more minutes taking the tree into the house and helping the girls secure it in the stand with Jo the whole time talking apparently casually about the waste of cut trees and how the world was losing oxygen and money frivolously spent on nonessentials.

"So, Little Angel," Jo said to Charlie, who was happily playing around the tree with her dolls. "Did you get a Santa pencil topper this morning?"

"Yes," said Charlie.

There was a pause while Jo looked stricken. Fiona, watching her, could see she was wondering if she'd made a mistake about which pockets she'd placed the Santas in.

"You got a Santa?" Jo repeated as if perhaps she'd heard wrong.

"Yes," said Charlie. "Fiona gave it to me."

"I see," said Jo.

There was a pause while Marlin looked at Jo triumphantly and Al, who was busy adjusting the tree in the stand some more, looked up suddenly alert.

"Well, I guess the question I was really asking was did you find a Santa pencil topper in *your* pocket?"

"No," said Charlie.

"And do you know why?" asked Jo.

"Because you didn't put it there," said Charlie.

"Because *Santa* didn't put it there," corrected Jo. "Because *Santa* doesn't give pencil toppers to children who don't believe in him."

"Fiona and Marlin and Natasha don't believe in Santa," said Charlie logically.

"Fiona and Marlin and Natasha are cynics, not Little Angels. Santa has given up on them," said Jo desperately.

This was so ridiculous, so illogical even for Jo, that Fiona burst into laughter.

Jo started to mutter but suddenly the tree that Al was adjusting crashed sideways into the wall and in the fuss of cleaning up the spilled water from the stand and keeping the lights away from it and relighting the tree, Jo's comments were lost. When the tree was back up, Al said, "All right, I'm back to work. Fiona, you want to come out to the trailer for a second?"

Fiona followed Al out, thinking he wanted to discuss their plans for Walmart, but instead he said, "So what was all this crap about some people getting Santas and Charlie not?"

Fiona told him the story. At the end Al said, "That woman has got to go. Between the two of us, Fiona, we can pretty much keep this family on track but not if you're going to ignore every bit of advice I give you. Particularly about *that* woman!" He went into his trailer and slammed the door with more than his usual vengeance.

Fiona stared at the door. Between the *two* of them? *This family?*

Fiona went back inside and found Mrs. Weatherspoon in the office typing emails to new church members. She closed the door behind her and then told Mrs. Weatherspoon about the Santa pencil toppers.

"Wasn't it nice of Jo to plan a little treat like that?" said

Mrs. Weatherspoon, her mind clearly more on her letter than on Fiona's story.

"But she didn't give one to Charlie on purpose," said Fiona.

"Well, perhaps she was proving a principle," said Mrs. Weatherspoon, still typing.

"What principle?" said Fiona. "She made Charlie cry."

"Charlie shouldn't take these things so seriously," said Mrs. Weatherspoon. "Tell me, do you think it's too early to think about a Sunday school?"

Fiona looked at her in disbelief. She didn't know how to answer but Mrs. Weatherspoon didn't bother waiting for an answer. "You know," she said as if Fiona had replied, "I think I'll ask how everyone feels about that. Jo would make a wonderful Sunday school teacher, don't you think?"

"Jo?" said Fiona, floundering for a way to say it. "Well, I think maybe there is something not quite right with Jo."

Mrs. Weatherspoon stopped typing finally and looked up. "Is it her arthritis again?"

"No, I mean mentally. Spiritually, if you like."

Mrs. Weatherspoon snorted derisively. "Nonsense. Jo has had dreadful troubles in her life and is handling them bravely. We could all learn from Jo."

Suddenly, thought Fiona, she appeared to be Fiona in Wonderland, with Al talking as if the two of them were running the family and the idea of Jo being someone they could all learn from. *Where is Tweedledee? Where is Tweedledum?* she was thinking, when one of the cats, which had been on top of a cabinet, landed on her head and scrambled off, scratching her neck.

"OUCH!" she cried out.

"Oh, aren't those cats cute?" said Jo, coming into the room. "They're always doing the most adorable things."

The Accident

Everyone became super busy as Christmas approached. Charlie checked under the tree every day to see if any presents had somehow magically appeared.

Natasha was being politely hounded by Mrs. Meyer to reconsider being in the school concert and amaze everyone even if she didn't want to continue studying violin.

"At least think about it," she beseeched Natasha, but Natasha flatly refused.

Mrs. Dennison had announced that the plays would all be performed at the big holiday concert but now Marlin didn't mind. Jeannie told her that Ted wasn't being pinched although he would still be thrown out into the arctic snows. And the fart joke had been removed. Mostly because Mrs. Dennison had heard about it and was not amused. So the last impediment keeping Marlin from feeling one hundred percent happy about her situation—that it might put Ted in a worse one—had been eliminated. And best of all, she and Jeannie, so unlike each other, had yet clicked in that magical way that defies explanation.

Marlin thought back to September, when she had scanned the faces of the girls in front of the school looking for someone smart enough or interesting enough to be her friend and marveled that it had never occurred to her to include kindness on that list of attributes. And the more she saw of Jeannie's kindness, the more she saw it as a particular kind of intelligence. An ability to see things clearly and still navigate the world without becoming lost to it.

Fiona was becoming a little frantic because Al kept putting off going to Walmart. She wondered again if maybe she should ask Mrs. Weatherspoon to take her after all so that they could finally hang some ornaments on the tree but that would mean the inclusion of Jo and Jo was such a killjoy she couldn't stand the thought of having Jo traipse around behind her, making comments about everything she purchased, from evil sugar to evil plastic to evil big-box stores. So she waited as patiently as she could but every night she twisted and turned in bed wishing they could get the ornaments up and the stockings hung soon, knowing that the lead-up to Christmas was half the fun.

Charlie kept asking when the presents would go under the tree. One day on the bus ride home from school she brought it up again. "Ashley says all their presents are under the tree already."

"I thought she believed in Santa," said Natasha.

"Her mother says Santa drops off the presents early at her house to avoid the Christmas rush," said Charlie.

"Oh, for God's sake," said Marlin, rolling her eyes. "Does he wrap them at her house too?"

Wrapping paper, thought Fiona. That was another thing she needed.

Fiona had said nothing to anyone but she had been crocheting everyone toques for their present this year. She had an easy pattern and had planned this all the way back in August, when she had secretly bought a variety of yarn in different colors. She had been working on them on the porch swing when the weather was nice, and because Fiona often had some crocheting in her hands, no one had shown much interest. She had done a pink fuzzy one for Charlie, a royal-blue one out of chunky yarn for Marlin, a green one for Natasha so she could blend in with the trees, a brown wool one for Al, and a mauve one for herself. A toque didn't require much yarn and she had more than enough to spare for multicolored ones out of the leftover colors for Mrs. Weatherspoon and Jo. Although it riled her to make one for Jo. The feelings of ill will toward Jo and how she had managed to secure Mrs. Weatherspoon to her team roiled up within Fiona day and night. A dark volcano of hatred that colored everything. It was a torturous feeling that Jo inspired and no matter how hard she tried, Fiona couldn't extricate herself from it. Instead, like acid, it ate away at her being.

"I think we should get Al something special," said Charlie.

"Why?" asked Fiona. "I already have something for him, which I can't tell you about because everyone is getting the same thing this year."

"But I think we should get him something extra because he adopted us," said Charlie. "If it weren't for him, we'd be in different families. I think he should get a special thank-you Christmas present."

Fiona was surprised. It was unlike Charlie to think of other people this way.

"You know," Fiona said, "I think you're right. We *should* get him something special. From all of us. But what?"

"A bear?" said Charlie. "A stuffed bear? To remind him of Billy. I could help him take care of it. Maybe I could even keep it on my bed for him."

This, thought Fiona, sounded more like Charlie.

"I don't know," said Marlin. "He doesn't seem like the stuffed animal sort."

"Something he would like," suggested Natasha.

"Well, obviously something he would *like*," said Marlin. "We wouldn't give him something we thought he wouldn't like. The question is what?"

"Let's all think about it," said Fiona. "And let me know if you have an idea. He's supposed to take me to Shoreline soon to do the shopping."

"It's getting close to Christmas," said Charlie. "Jo says we have to go to Shoreline on Christmas morning for the first service at the new church. It's only going to be in the Simmonses' basement but she said the surroundings don't matter. And she said we all have to attend Jo's Sunday school."

Marlin gave Fiona a significant look. "Fiona and I are too old for Sunday school. And maybe Jo and Mrs. Weatherspoon will be gone before then anyway."

Fiona thought about it all day during school. How to get Mrs. Weatherspoon to see what Jo really was and get her to ditch Jo, thus winning at least one small victory. And after that, how to get rid of both of them without being rude. She was thinking about it so hard that she missed two of the questions Mr. Byrne asked her when he called upon her in class but instead of his usual teasing manner, he seemed preoccupied and only partly present. At the end of class she found out why.

"Now," Mr. Byrne said ten minutes before the bell. "Before you all go running to your rides I have an announcement. I have loved my time on Pine Island. I have loved teaching this class. Some of you in particular." And here he looked straight into Fiona's eyes. "But my father had a heart attack last night. I'm leaving for the mainland on the last ferry tonight. I'm going to care for him in Vancouver over the holidays and then my family and I are moving him back to Ireland. He's eighty-two and he wishes to spend the rest of his life there and we've decided to go back as well so we can care for him. Believe me, I wouldn't have taken this job had I known my time here would be so short and cause such an interruption in everyone's studies." He paused a moment as if hoping better words would come to him and when they didn't, finished, "So this was our last class together. Tomorrow you'll have a new teacher named Ms. Grady. I hope you'll afford her all the respect and all the joy you've afforded me."

Beth in the back row began clapping and the whole class took it up. Then the bell rang and everyone ran for their backpacks and coats shouting merry Christmas and good luck and thank you to Mr. Byrne as they left.

If Mr. Byrne was her friend, thought Fiona, if he felt the friendship as keenly as she had, a kindred spirit, why had he not told her he was leaving before? Was their friendship all in her own head? Was she just another student? She had sometimes wondered this.

Fiona started out the door, deciding that the friendship she'd thought they had, the excitement of the meeting of their sharp minds, was on her part alone, and not wanting to claim special status and too shocked by his announcement to process it fully, but Mr. Byrne called her back.

"Fiona, don't go!" he called, and she pushed back into the classroom and waited until the last student left.

Then he said quietly, "I have something for you."

He handed her a small leather-bound copy of Word-sworth.

"I brought it here from Scotland. I want you to have it," he said.

Fiona didn't know what to say but she wanted to say something. Something that would show how important he had been to her. How in him, despite the age differ-ence, she had found a like spirit and how it had given her hope that the world was not just full of people like Jo, not just full of ordinary people, but every so often you met one who made the world a more exciting, a more beautiful place. "Thank you…" Fiona paused. This would be the last time she ever saw him, most likely. She wanted to tell him how much his friendship had mattered and she meant to say it in a measured way but to her horror what she sud-denly blurted out was "I love you."

Mr. Byrne looked startled, then slightly aghast as if he needed to have the right answer to this and didn't. As if, had someone come into the room at that moment, he cared what they would think, so he said, "That's nice," in a kind voice. It was the kindness he injected into his voice that humiliated Fiona. It was horrible that she had said "I love you." As soon as it was out of her mouth she had wanted to ratchet it back. She *did* love him, she real-ized, but you didn't *say* such a thing. Not to a teacher. But his response was even worse. It underlined what a stupid thing it had been to say. She sounded like a lovestruck idiot. She blushed to her hairline, turned around, and ran.

She sped furiously to the parking lot, hoping to leap onto the bus before Mr. Byrne, perhaps, came after her, but to add misery to humiliation, she found that the school bus had already left and she would have a long rainy walk ahead of her.

She continued to hurry out of the parking lot and away from the school and had begun the long plod home when a car pulled up and a window rolled down.

"Want a ride?" asked Davy Clement.

Fiona didn't think twice but ran around to the passenger side and hopped in.

"Should I take you home?" asked Davy.

"Thanks," said Fiona. "I missed the bus."

"So I see," said Davy. "This direction down Farhill Road, right?"

She nodded and he started toward her house.

"I guess you got your license," she said.

"My learner's," he said, smiling. Even with just his profile she could see his eyes twinkle.

"And now your family let you have the car?"

"My parents are in Calgary for a week. I'm manning the fort with my brothers and sisters and one of the perks is I get the car when my older sister, who's supposed to be in charge, isn't using it. But she hardly ever does. She bikes into work in St. Mary's so it mostly just sits in the garage so I took it to school today. I was going to go to Shoreline and maybe have supper there. Maybe a hot dog at Dairy Queen. My sister is cooking dinner all week but she's a lousy cook."

They drove in silence for a moment and then Fiona said, "Wait a second, can I come with you?"

"To Shoreline?"

"Do you mind? Do you have time? I have Christmas shopping I need to do at Walmart. It might take me an hour. You could drop me off while you go to Dairy Queen. Or is that too much?"

"Nah, I got nothing else to do and my brothers will just be home wrestling and ripping the house to shreds anyway. The longer I stay away, the better."

"Won't your sister worry if you're gone so long?"

"She never worries."

"Lucky her," said Fiona.

Davy turned the car around and they drove down the road toward Shoreline. For a while they said nothing and then Fiona said, "Won't Maisie mind if she finds out you took me with you to Shoreline?"

There was a silence and then Davy said, "We kind of broke up last week."

"Oh," said Fiona. "I'm sorry."

"She wasn't really the right person for me. I should have seen it but…" He shrugged.

Fiona wanted to say, *It's hard to see anything with your tongue stuck down someone's throat,* but she kept quiet.

Presently he said, "Hey, maybe I'll come to Walmart with you. I want to get some stuff too. I haven't done any Christmas shopping."

"Oh, shoot," said Fiona. "I've been preoccupied with something and now I realize they're going to wonder at home why I missed the bus and where I am. I'd better phone. You haven't gotten a cell phone since last spring, have you?"

"No, but don't worry, there're still pay phones in the Walmart entranceway. I've got a loonie you can use to call from there."

"Thanks, I've got a loonie, though."

Fiona settled down comfortably in her seat after that and Davy sped into Shoreline, driving much faster than Al and, thought Fiona uncomfortably, somewhat erratically.

It partly gave Fiona a thrill and partly terrified her but they made the trip in record time.

Fiona called home and told Marlin where she was and that Davy had his learner's permit and his family's car.

Marlin said, "It's a good thing you called. Charlie told Al you didn't come home and he's pacing around outside trying to decide whether to drive to the school and look for you. I'll tell him Davy picked you up. Where's Maisie?"

"Not here," said Fiona, not going into detail because Davy was standing close by.

"So it's just the two of you?"

"Uh-huh," said Fiona.

"No chaperone?" teased Marlin. "Is this like a date?"

"Nope," said Fiona. "Definitely not. Listen, I have to go. We're shopping at Walmart and then going to Dairy Queen. Davy wants a hot dog."

"Too bad you can't bring Al back one for Christmas. He loves Dairy Queen."

"Wait a second, that's a great idea," said Fiona.

"What? I was kidding."

"Not a hot dog. We could get him a Dairy Queen ice cream cake! All his own. With something written on it, like Merry Christmas and all our names. We could store it in the freezer. He never goes there."

There was a second while Marlin considered this and then she said, "You know, that's pretty much the perfect present. Do it."

"I will. Just don't tell Charlie. She'll never keep the secret."

Fiona hung up and repeated the conversation to Davy. Then she stopped herself.

"Well, shoot," she said. "It won't work. The cake will melt on the way home."

"Not if you're willing to spend a bit more money," said

Davy. "Walmart sells those insulated bags for frozen food and ice. My mom uses hers when she comes in for a big shop so things don't defrost on the way home."

Fiona was so grateful for his solution that she gave Davy's arm a little squeeze. His eyes lit up briefly and they headed into the store.

Meanwhile Marlin ran outside to tell Al.

"Wait, how old is this Davy? I thought he was just a year older than Fiona," said Al after his initial relief. "So how did he get his license so fast?"

"She said he has his learner's," said Marlin. "He gave Fiona a lift to Walmart."

"Is there an adult with them?"

"No, just the two of them," said Marlin. "But don't worry, Fiona said it wasn't, like, a date. They're just friends now apparently."

"There's *just the two of them*?" shouted Al. "He has to have a licensed adult driver in the car with him! He's learning! That's what a learner's is. Are you sure there's no one else there?"

"Well, no," said Marlin, regretting spilling the beans. "But I guess it's all right with his parents because they gave him the family car."

"All *right*? All *right*?" shouted Al. "Listen, Marlin, it is not *all right*! I'm going to go find them. For one thing, what he's doing is illegal. Where are his parents, that's what I'd like to know! They can let him risk his own neck all they like but they have no right to risk Fiona's! Where did Fiona say they were going?"

"Walmart and Dairy Queen."

"Walmart and Dairy Queen!" spat out Al, as if those two places proved his point.

"Dairy Queen?" said Charlie, who had been watching this whole interaction with interest from the porch steps. "Can I come?"

"No!" shouted Al, and got in his truck and took off.

Charlie began to tear up.

"He's not mad at you, Charlie," said Marlin. "He's mad at Davy. And maybe Fiona."

"I wanted to go to Dairy Queen," said Charlie.

"Well, cheer up," said Marlin. "Maybe Jo has a recipe for a yummy sugar-free lentil ice cream."

<hr />

Despite the terrible end to the school day, Walmart worked a certain magic, so full of wonderful cheap Christmas tat was it, with cheesy carols blasting forth all over the store. Suddenly Fiona was full of the Christmas spirit. She and Davy grabbed baskets and strolled up and down aisles, filling them with presents and stocking stuffers and decorations.

"So who's doing *your* stocking?" asked Davy.

"Me, I guess," said Fiona.

"Aw, that's no good," said Davy.

"Really, it's fine," said Fiona. "At least I will like what I'm getting."

"I'll tell you what. What are you spending on each stocking?"

"I don't know. About thirty bucks, I guess."

"Okay, give me the thirty bucks or give me your credit card and I'll do yours."

"Oh, you don't have to do that," said Fiona. "I mean, I don't like to sound mean but you wouldn't even know what to get me."

"Sure I would. I have sisters," he said. "Come on. It will be more fun for you if you're surprised too."

So Fiona peeled off a ten and a twenty from the money in her wallet and they split up.

She bought everyone fancy pens and chocolate Santas. She bought Marlin chocolate-covered cherries and a bath bomb. She got Charlie some fashion doll dresses and accessories. She bought Natasha a bird whistle and Crazy Eights. Everyone got socks. She had so much fun and it came at such a good time, after the horrible good-bye with Mr. Byrne, that she was doubly grateful to Davy.

When they met after the checkout, on the dregs of all the adrenaline of the afternoon, she felt punchy. She twinkled and joked and punched his arm jocularly. They carried the bags out to the car, laughing at stupid jokes and trying to decide which exiting Santa-hat-clad shopper looked the most ridiculous. Then they went to Dairy Queen, where Fiona picked out the most ornate ice cream cake they had. She had them write *Merry Christmas, From Fiona, Marlin, Natasha, and Charlie* on it. After that Davy insisted on treating her to a hot dog and Fiona put the ice cream cake in the insulated bag with the ice and they headed home.

At five o'clock it was already pitch black, cold and rainy. There were no streetlights once they left Shoreline and headed down the long road to St. Mary's By the Sea. Fiona thought it was fortunate that there was little traffic as well because the street was icy and more than once Davy skidded dangerously over the center line.

The first two times this happened Fiona squawked, "Be careful! Slow down." And for a while Davy would and then his foot would become heavier and heavier and the car would begin to go too quickly again.

The third time it happened the car skidded, did a donut, and in sickening slow motion glided to the ditch and did a half turn before sliding down the side and landing at the bottom of it. Fortunately, right side up.

For several moments neither of them said anything. Fiona was breathing hard and slowly released her viselike grip on the door arm, saying tersely, "Now what?"

"Aren't you going to ask if I'm all right?" asked Davy.

"You were going too fast," Fiona spat out. "I warned you. You could have killed us."

"I guess we'll have to wait here in the car until we see lights. It's so dark we should be able to see a car coming from far away and get out to the road to flag it down before it gets here."

"Oh, good plan," said Fiona sarcastically. "Thank goodness you can think ahead so wisely."

Davy looked chastened. "Look, I'm sorry, okay? I didn't *want* this to happen."

As they waited for approaching car lights and the heat of the car died down, they began to feel the cold through their coats. Rain and sleet poured down in great sheets outside.

"At least it's dry in the car," said Davy.

"I'm freezing," said Fiona, shivering.

"Let's get in the backseat under the blanket there," suggested Davy. "It's kind of gross. It's the dog blanket. But at least it will be warm."

Fiona nodded and she and Davy crawled over the center console to the backseat to save going out and getting wetter in the rain. They pressed themselves together for body heat and Davy wrapped the blanket around the two of them.

"I'm really, really sorry, for everything. I mean it,

Fiona, for the car, for Maisie, for everything," Davy began, and then before Fiona knew it, he had put his arm around her shoulder and was pulling her in closer.

She pushed him quickly away and said, "Hey! I don't want that!"

It wasn't very eloquent but it did the trick. He looked as if she'd struck him.

"Well, gee, you were acting before like we were back together, joking and punching my arm," he said.

"Listen, I was grateful but it doesn't mean we're more than friends."

"Well, why did you come into town with me?"

"I needed a *lift*. A *lift*. I wasn't looking for anything else. What did you think? That the second you discarded Maisie, there I would be waiting? That I'd been *pining* for you?"

"We were having a good time!" said Davy.

"Yes, as *friends*."

"When we were laughing outside Walmart I thought it was almost like a date. I thought we were back together. How was I supposed to know you didn't feel that way?"

"You weren't," said Fiona, beginning to calm down, realizing she'd been sending mixed signals. "But now you do."

"Fiona," said Davy, also beginning to calm down, "I don't know why you stood me up last spring. I was mad all summer. I think I started going out with Maisie even though I really didn't like her that much because I was mad at you. But I'm over that."

Fiona, listening to this, thought how little she cared now. She didn't care about Maisie or what had happened. It all seemed so juvenile, really, compared to the kind of thing she knew she wanted someday. The kind of meeting of the minds she had had with Mr. Byrne. Davy was nice but she couldn't imagine having the kind of talks with him she had had on paper with Mr. Byrne.

"I'm sorry," she said. "I wanted to say I was sorry in the fall for standing you up but you were with Maisie so it seemed kind of pointless. I didn't stand you up on purpose anyhow. Something came up. Something I can't really talk about. I sent my sister to tell you but you were gone."

"I know. Someone told me your sister had come but I was still mad. But I'm not anymore." He looked at her beseechingly. He leaned in slightly and started to put his arm around her again but she scooted away a few inches.

"The thing is, I'm over it now too," she said.

"What do you mean? You mean you just don't like me that way anymore?" He looked appalled.

Fiona thought how she had been appalled in the fall when she first caught sight of him with Maisie. How it had never occurred to her that he would simply move on.

And now he was having that same realization about her. She felt sorry for him because she knew what that kind of bafflement felt like but she couldn't pretend to things she didn't honestly feel.

"I'm sorry," she said.

Davy's face turned stony and although they shared the blanket after that he was scrupulous not to have any part of him touching her. She sighed. It all felt unnecessarily dramatic. She grew colder and colder and all she wanted to do was go home but they hadn't seen a single car and she wondered what they would think at home when she didn't arrive. Would they come looking for her? Would they call the police?

It was just as she was thinking this that they saw car lights in the distance coming from the direction of Shoreline. "Come on," said Davy. "Let's both leap up and down and wave our arms and hope they spot us in the dark."

"Turn the car lights back on," said Fiona. "So they can see there's a car in the ditch. I'll start waving my arms."

She stepped out into the sleet, which was still coming down in buckets and immediately soaked her hair. As she waved her arms, she noticed that the car lights approaching were too high for an ordinary car. *Truck,* she thought. And then a second later, as it slowed and she got a closer look, *Oh my God. Miracle. Not just any truck. Al's! Al!* She started shrieking, "Al! Al!"

Al pulled over and leapt out. "Are you all right?" he shouted, running over. "I was looking all over Shoreline for you!"

"Yes, we're fine. The car skidded into the ditch!" said Fiona, practically in tears, so relieved was she.

"Where is that little weasel?" shouted Al.

"What?" said Fiona, startled.

"And what's the matter with you, I thought you were a bright girl. What kind of lunatic gets into a car with someone who doesn't know how to drive? On a dark and icy night?"

"We…" began Fiona.

"Get in the truck!" ordered Al.

"I have to get my stuff," said Fiona.

"Then get your stuff and get into the truck. And you," said Al to Davy, who was trying to climb up the side of the ditch back to the road. "I'm taking you home and having a word with your parents. They can figure out how to get this thing towed."

"My parents are in Calgary," said Davy, his teeth chattering.

Fiona grabbed all her bags and her backpack and climbed into the truck and then Davy squished in next to her.

"It wasn't really his fault totally," began Fiona.

"Be quiet," ordered Al. "Do you have any idea how worried I've been?"

"The roads were—" began Davy.

"You *really* be quiet, do you understand?" barked Al.

Davy nodded, still shivering. It was very quiet the rest of the way to Davy's house.

Davy directed Al down his street and Al pulled into his driveway and went with a nervous Davy to his front door, barking over his shoulder at Fiona, "Stay in the truck."

From the truck Fiona could hear Al talking to Davy's sister, who had come to the door, and then she heard Davy's sister shouting at Davy. Al came back to the truck and got in silently.

"What are you doing now?" asked Fiona nervously because it was clear Al was still seething. "You aren't calling the police or anything, are you?"

"No, his sister didn't even *know* he had taken the car out, Fiona. She hadn't thought to check the garage. So she just thought Davy was out with friends somewhere. You heard her shouting. He's in enough trouble as it is. But where were *your* brains! Getting into a car with someone who only has his learner's permit? Are you *crazy*! Didn't you know he was supposed to have a licensed adult with him to drive?"

"I *didn't* know!" shouted Fiona back. And then the whole long crazy day came crashing down around her ears and she started sobbing in great gulps and once she started she couldn't stop.

Al drove silently for a bit and then he sighed. "Look,

I'm sorry for shouting. I guess you didn't know. You probably haven't been here long enough to know the ins and outs of licenses. But you'd think you'd have at least *heard* what the laws were here. Don't your friends talk?" he began, but as this seemed to be making Fiona sob all the louder, he stopped. When she hadn't stopped hysterically gulping and sobbing after a few blocks he said, "What is it? Are you in love with this guy or something?"

"Oh GOD no!" said Fiona so emphatically between sobs that Al almost laughed but restrained himself.

"Then *what?* Oh, I know, it's *that woman*! That horrible woman, isn't it?"

"What horrible woman?" sobbed Fiona.

"Jo," said Al. "How many horrible women do you know?"

"It's not that, it's *everything*," sobbed Fiona, thinking mostly of her horrible good-bye with Mr. Byrne and her humiliation.

Al kept saying, "What? What? Calm down, I can't understand you."

"Never mind, it's all horrible, horrible," she spluttered incoherently.

After that Fiona lapsed back into sniffling. Al became thoughtful and parked the truck.

"Well, let me help you," he had begun to say, when Fiona shouted, "NO ONE CAN HELP ME!", grabbed her bags, and ran sobbing again into the house.

Marlin, who'd been waiting on the porch in the rain, said, "What happened?"

"I'll be darned if I know!" snapped Al. "I'm sending this whole family for therapy first chance I get. Starting with *her*!"

And he went slamming into his trailer.

"Well, well, quite the little drama we have going," said Marlin to no one, for now she was alone on the porch.

And she went inside to try to get the whole story from Fiona.

Christmas Surprises

For several days afterward, Fiona and Al were awkward with each other and Al, particularly, seemed to be in a dark mood. But then Christmas was almost upon them and a switch seemed to have been flicked in Al and his mood lightened and finally turned to downright buoyancy. The girls caught him whistling to himself frequently and singing snippets of "Holly Jolly Christmas."

"I wouldn't have thought he was the holiday sort, would you have?" Marlin asked Fiona as they watched him cutting firewood for the girls' fireplace. He had had someone in to clean the chimney so the girls could start making fires for the holidays.

"No, but these days nothing surprises me," said Fiona, whose spirits had also risen as Christmas approached.

The Dairy Queen cake had stayed nicely intact and frozen and Fiona had put it in the freezer under a load of bread, where she hoped, if for some odd reason Al did go into the freezer, it would remain hidden. She had stuffed and hidden the three stockings in her room and Marlin had taken Davy's purchases and stuffed and hidden Fiona's. It was beginning to feel like a house full of happy secrets.

At the end of the week was the holiday concert, with Marlin and Charlie both taking part. Marlin with Jeannie was one of the trees in her group's play and Charlie was a sheep in her class's rendition of "Silent Night," sung, for no reason anyone could figure out, by farm animals. Natasha, of course, would not be performing with the strings group. And Fiona's class was also not involved because they, like the classes not taking part, would be doing the spring concert instead, so she and Natasha would be sitting with Al and Mrs. Weatherspoon and Jo.

Charlie began to hop around the house, pretending to search for presents as Christmas approached.

"You ninny," said Marlin. "It's Christmas, not Easter, with an Easter egg hunt. We're not *hiding* the presents."

"When are they going under the tree?" asked Charlie impatiently, so Fiona wrapped all the toques and put them under the tree with the gift tags Charlie had made. Charlie picked hers up every morning and squeezed it, trying to guess what it was.

Jeannie was helping Marlin do something for everyone for Christmas. Marlin had gone to her house after school for several days and one day brought home seven lumpy packages, which she put under the tree.

"Well, what happened to one present for everyone?" Fiona wanted to know.

"As you said," said Marlin, "Mom and Dad aren't here anymore. We may have to adjust a few traditions."

Marlin was in the kitchen every day too. She put up with Jo's passive-aggressive comments and attempts to take over the oven and edge Marlin out and pushed back in a way that was more the Marlin everyone knew and loved. Marlin slaved over Christmas cookies of many varieties and plates of them were sprinkled around the house. The only downside was the kittens, who got into them if they didn't remember to replace the Saran Wrap on top of the plates. The kittens also managed to tip the tree several times and despite being warm and cuddly didn't get a lot of attention from anyone but Jo.

"I just don't like cats," Fiona admitted as she cleaned a wound from one of the many places the kittens let loose their claws as she tried to keep them out of the cookies.

"I hate the litter box," said Marlin. "You need to tell Mrs. Weatherspoon that before she and Jo leave they have to find new homes for the cats. No one likes them and it's not fair to keep them around letting them get attached to us."

"I don't think those cats will attach to anyone," said Fiona, as one defied her words literally by leaping onto her shoulders and digging in its claws again. "And vice versa." She put it gently on the floor.

"Maybe we should auction them off at the concert," joked Marlin. "Three more days to the concert and then a glorious two-week vacation!"

The night of the holiday concert, Al came into the house to eat with everyone. He retained his buoyant good mood and when it was time for dessert, passed out candy canes.

"Hmmm," said Jo in her disapproving way, miffed that no one was eating her dates stuffed with silken tofu. "Hmmm." But that was all she said.

Mrs. Weatherspoon drove Jo, Fiona, Marlin, and Natasha to the school. Charlie went with Al in his truck. Charlie had on the sheep costume that Mrs. Weatherspoon had made and went to her classroom to prepare for the concert and Marlin left everyone when they got there to find Jeannie and their greenroom. Everyone in the concert was either backstage or in the classrooms close to the auditorium to wait their turn onstage.

Al, Fiona, Natasha, Mrs. Weatherspoon, and Jo went to the auditorium, where they found good seats near the front.

"These chairs are so *hard,*" complained Jo.

Al laughed and this seemed to infuriate Jo, who pursed her lips and moved farther from him, to the other side of Mrs. Weatherspoon, where she plunked herself down and tapped her foot impatiently, saying she wished these things could start *occasionally* on time.

The concert was lovely, full of the usual mishaps that only make such concerts dearer. During intermission, Mrs. Meyer surprised them by coming up and greeting Al and then turning to Natasha and saying, "Natasha, we're having a bit of an emergency. Our solo violinist has gone home with a tummy upset so we have a big hole in the concert piece. I know you could pick up the part in a moment. Would you consider stepping in?"

Natasha, who was sitting between Fiona and Al, slumped back in her seat as if she wished it would swallow her up and shook her head.

"Please?" begged Mrs. Meyer. "I wouldn't ask you, but it's really an emergency."

"No," said Natasha.

"Now, Natasha, you little weirdo," said Jo. "If it were me and I had a chance to save the school concert, I would always say yes. I don't think you have a choice."

"Well," said Mrs. Meyer uncomfortably, "I wouldn't say *that*…"

Natasha looked panicked.

"You certainly have a choice, Natasha. But please, just this once?" beseeched Mrs. Meyer

"Get up there and do your bit!" exhorted Jo.

"No," whispered Natasha.

"That's it," said Al. "The answer is no. No, ladies, is a

complete sentence. Now, where are people getting that hot chocolate?"

For some of the audience was now drifting back into the auditorium carrying paper cups of steaming liquid, cookies, and napkins. Al stood up and Natasha stood up beside him, and Fiona noticed in shock that Natasha, of her own volition, put her hand in Al's and they ambled off.

"Well, I think that stinks," said Jo, turning to find Mrs. Weatherspoon already gone to look for the hot chocolate and cookies. "It's one thing to be a little weirdo but it's another to be an uncooperative one."

"Oh, no, really, it's fine, I can always play it myself, I'd just hoped for a student, it is a student concert, after all," murmured Mrs. Meyer, looking slightly distressed because she could see she had upset Natasha. She scuttled off. Fiona gave Jo a long look and went out to find Al and Natasha.

As Fiona went down the hall she saw a long table set up with a sign on the wall above it saying HERO TABLE. She stopped for a second to glimpse the medal and trophy that Charlie had brought in and the little cards behind the photos of their parents with a favorite quote of each of them.

A minute later Marlin was behind her. "So there they are—the old Fresno Bowling Champs!"

She was about to read aloud the two quotes in Charlie's uneven printing when Jo was suddenly behind the girls.

"Your sister is such a little *weirdo*!" she said in a voice loud enough to be heard by everyone passing by. "Did Fiona tell you she wouldn't even play the violin to help out the concert? If you ask me she needs a psychiatrist."

Marlin turned on her. All her pent-up rage accumulated over the last few months boiled over and she became incoherent with hatred. "You...you SHUT UP!" she whispered, balling her hands into fists. "You...you just SHUT UP! JUST SHUT UP! You horrible horrible person, just just SHUT UP!"

Jo didn't even flinch. A small satisfied smile creased her face and she said to no one in particular, "I told Tildy that you'd all end up like this, rude, feral weirdos, being raised by that crazy man. Well, I guess I was right. You can't say I didn't do my best to save Charlie but even she is a lost cause." And she turned and sauntered back to the auditorium.

Marlin was left shaking, staring after her.

"Calm down," said Fiona, who was shaking too. "Well, that was about as rude as you could get so I hope it made you feel better."

"No," said Marlin. "I mean it felt deliciously bad like eating only ice cream for dinner but now I feel sick. And she didn't even *care*, did you see that? If anything, she was gloating that she made me explode. I think she was actually *glad* to make me angry, to make me as sick and nasty as she is. I feel so stupid, so stupid to let her do that to me!"

How will I live in the world? thought Marlin. *It's like I can't stand anyone anymore. I can see who these people are, Jo, the mean girls and Georgia, Mrs. Dennison, even that horrible side of Mrs. Weatherspoon, and then I can't stand them. I can't live with these violent feelings of anger all the time that come in waves. Al is right, there will always be people like this around.* "Fiona, maybe the problem isn't Jo. Maybe the problem is me."

"Are you kidding? The problem is definitely Jo. Just get a breath. Come on, we'll pretend to be interested in the hero table until you can pull yourself together."

The girls walked the length of the table, reading the quotes, until Marlin felt her blood pressure begin to drop. Then she read the quotes Charlie had written for her parents in her uneven printing. "Don't rain on anyone's parade." And "When you see a special light in someone else, it not only reaffirms that such light exists, but once more you find your own."

"If that's true," said Marlin still in a shaky voice, "then the opposite is true. That seeing someone like Jo with horribleness radiating from them is all we need to find that place in ourselves. It's why we don't want to be around them, because it brings out that side of ourselves."

"Yes, yes, no doubt," said Fiona hurriedly. She was still afraid of what Marlin would do next. "Daddy used to treat everyone with the same respect. Remember that? Even people he couldn't stand he could somehow manage to treat kindly."

"I know," said Marlin. "But Fiona, I can't help it. I feel like I'm locked in battle with so many people I can't stand. Someone has to change, them or me. And it's not going to be me."

Fiona thought back. "Mr. Byrne once said that writing a journal wasn't about changing yourself. It's about getting to know who you really are. Maybe who you are is just fine, you just have to find out who that really is."

This had never occurred to Marlin and now it was as if a door opened. What if she was so furious with these people because she saw things as either-or, either she would have to change or they would, either they were right or she was. And she was intent on them being the ones to change. What if she didn't have to get them to change any more than she had to change herself?

"Fiona, what if the reason I'm so mad is that I can't get any of these people to change? Jo or Mrs. Weatherspoon? What if that wasn't up to us?"

"What are you saying? That we have to be more tolerant or something?"

"No." Marlin stopped to puzzle this out. "No, I mean

what if we don't have to change *them* but we don't have to let them change us either?"

"So what are we left with?" asked Fiona, who couldn't completely follow.

As she said this Jeannie Eisenberg came down the hall toward them to get Marlin. Marlin thought how unabashedly herself Jeannie was. And the freedom it seemed to give her.

"Fiona, if we don't have to change either then it's okay to dislike Jo. And we don't have to change Jo so that we *do* like her. We just have to *get rid of her*. Because it's okay not to like her. That's who we are. And she can be herself. That's who she is. But she needs to be herself *somewhere else*. It's not about tolerating these people by being a better person ourselves. It's not about making them be better people so we can tolerate them. It's not us versus them. It's everybody be who they are but avoid the people you don't like, hang out with the people you do. That simple."

"Come on," said Jeannie as she came up on Marlin. "We have to get back to the classroom and put our costumes on."

"Go ahead. I'll be there soon," said Marlin because thoughts were forming quickly now. And for Fiona too as the enormity of their revelation swam about her. They approached the auditorium, where Jo and Al stood talking to a parent as Natasha went back to her seat.

"How, though? We have no way to get rid of them. It's like when we said we didn't want to go to the new church. Mrs. Weatherspoon just vetoed us," said Fiona.

But even as she said that, a solution appeared, because they could hear Jo, talking to a parent, say in a loud voice, "Well, of course we wanted to see more of the country. By train. But we can't afford it. They've got us sleeping on this dinky couch that's ruining our backs. I'd be out of here like a shot if we could travel but oh well, houseguests must be content."

Al left Jo's side to join the girls just as Marlin said, "That's it! We could send them across the country on a train trip. It's win-win. They would WANT to go if they could, which they can if we pay for it. And boom, they're gone."

"Marlin, we don't have that kind of money!" said Fiona despairingly.

"What are you talking about?" asked Al.

"Getting rid of Jo and Mrs. Weatherspoon," Marlin said.

The lights in the hall flashed.

"I've got to get to my classroom," said Marlin.

"Think of something else. Something that doesn't cost so much!" begged Fiona again as Marlin took off, calling back, "There isn't anything. Think about it. It's perfect. It's worth every penny too!"

"So it's finally time to get rid of the houseguests?" said Al as he and Fiona filed back into the auditorium. "What caused this sea change?"

"It's so long and complicated I can't even begin to explain," said Fiona. "We had this perfect way to get rid of them, give them one-way train tickets across Canada, but it's not practical. We'll have to think again."

Al and Fiona found their seats and sat down just as Jo said, "Why couldn't they get more comfortable chairs? Do they really expect people to sit through a whole concert on these horrible folding wood contraptions? First that horrible bed, now these horrible chairs, does no one think about my back?"

"Well, gee, one-way train tickets, can't think why you'd give them those," said Al, laughing, as Jo continued to whine even as the curtain rose.

Fiona frowned, her mind frantically surveying their bank account and assets as the idea of train tickets continued to tempt her. But it was no good. She needed that money for their future.

Then they turned their attention to the stage, where the curtain had come all the way up and an elf was being heaved out into a pile of white sheets that were supposed to be a snowbank.

"That's what you get for hating toys!" cried Georgia.

"Slinky, slink *this*!" cried Ted the elf.

"Who writes this tripe?" whispered Al.

"Not Marlin," whispered Fiona.

"Shh," whispered the woman in the row behind.

And then everyone was quiet.

The next few days were lovely and lazy and then the pace changed the day before Christmas and the girls woke to an unusual bustle of activity. Mrs. Weatherspoon was on the phone and writing things down and shuffling through papers and Jo was doing loads of laundry.

While Marlin and Fiona made themselves breakfast, Mrs. Weatherspoon called from the office, "Now, girls, I'm putting together a file of information about the church for you. You will just love the new members, several of whom have children. They will need you to recruit more families with children and perhaps help to put together a youth group."

Marlin gave Fiona a hard look. She was supposed to tell Mrs. Weatherspoon in no uncertain terms that they would not be joining the church but Fiona had put this off.

Fiona buttered her toast and said, "Hmmm," noncommittally.

Marlin pinched her.

"Well, I didn't say yes," whispered Fiona.

"And all of you will be invaluable explaining missions," Mrs. Weatherspoon called out from the office.

"We told Carol Simmons that Al will take you to the service tomorrow," said Jo. "There will be two so you should be able to make the noon one. There's no pastor yet but communal prayer is key."

"Why would Al be taking us?" asked Marlin.

"I mean…" said Jo, and stopped in some confusion.

"Jo!" said Mrs. Weatherspoon more sharply than the girls had heard her before. She headed to the laundry room. "Come help me with this laundry basket, I swear, the older I get…"

Jo scuttled away to the laundry room with Mrs. Weatherspoon and there was the sound of much whispering.

"What's got into them?" Marlin asked Fiona.

"I don't know," said Fiona. "Excitement about the new church starting? Christmas? You don't suppose they have their own Christmas surprise for us?"

"Or they've finally tipped over into stark staring madness as we've all suspected they would," said Marlin.

"Well, I don't care. It's the holidays and I'm not doing anything but eating Christmas cookies and watching movies," said Fiona. "Even Jo can't ruin the day before Christmas for me."

And largely she didn't. Although it wasn't for lack of trying.

"Why is it that someone can't watch these cats? They've snagged my sweater, the one I want to wear tomorrow," said Jo.

Fiona's only answer was to fetch the kittens and take them to her room. She was not going to get drawn in. She was not going to get angry.

"And do we have to have that TV blaring when I'm trying to do things on the computer?" Jo called from the office. "With all the TV you girls watch, you will be completely brain-dead by the time you're adults."

Fiona sighed and turned down the television. She had to bite her lip several times to keep from saying something back to Jo. *She does not exist. She does not exist,* she thought. But unfortunately she did and it was still hard to tune her out. Why couldn't they think of a way to be rid of them that didn't involve so much money?

And then as the day wore on a small miracle occurred and Jo didn't seem interested in the girls anymore and her haranguing stopped. When Marlin said she was making pork roast for Christmas Eve, Jo shrugged and said fine, she wasn't cooking, there was some leftover lentil stew she would heat up for herself and Charlie. Even when Charlie announced that she thought she was done being vegan and would have pork roast instead, Jo didn't launch into one of her usual tirades about meat.

Al said he would come over for Christmas Day but would skip Christmas Eve so after a glorious stuffed pork roast with baked apples for dessert, all of which Marlin took photos of, the girls watched movies until bedtime, with Mrs. Weatherspoon patting their shoulders and generally behaving strangely each time she passed them on the couch.

Finally, the little girls headed up to bed. Marlin and Fiona hung the filled stockings from the mantel and then headed up too.

Later that night Fiona thought she heard noises downstairs and Al's big feet stomping up the porch steps and coming inside while she and Marlin were still reading in bed.

"Is that Al downstairs? What's he doing?" hissed Fiona.

"Oh, he probably has presents to put under the tree," said Marlin. "I'm pretty sure he wouldn't expect just to *get* presents. He's not like Jo."

"I notice Jo hasn't put anything under the tree but before you and I went upstairs Mrs. Weatherspoon did," said Fiona.

"I saw that too. They looked like books."

"That's what I thought."

"Probably religious tracts or Bible stories or some—" Marlin stopped midword. "Listen! Is that the car starting up outside?"

They listened for a second.

"Al must be going somewhere," said Fiona. "But where would he go on Christmas Eve?"

"Christmas is full of surprises," said Marlin happily.

But Christmas the next morning began more full of

surprise than even Marlin might have expected. To begin with, when the girls woke up Fiona found they had slept until seven-thirty. Fiona was used to being awakened by Jo feeding the kittens and starting her litany of morning complaints while she made the decaf coffee.

Instead Christmas morning there was a great silence in the house. And looking out the window, Fiona could see that during the night the weather had turned and snow had drifted down. It blanketed the lawn and was piled on the tree branches. She crept downstairs quietly so as not to wake Jo and Mrs. Weatherspoon, who must still be sleeping. To her surprise the couch was made up and Jo, Mrs. Weatherspoon, and the kittens were all gone.

At first she thought Mrs. Weatherspoon and Jo had decided to go into Shoreline for the earlier Christmas service but then she noticed that the suitcases that had been parked along a wall of the living room for months were also gone. She ran through the house to make sure they hadn't just been moved and when she found no sign of them she ran upstairs to wake Marlin.

"Marl! Marl! They're gone," she said to a sleepy Marlin, who was groaning in protest and rubbing her eyes.

"What do you mean? Who?" asked Marlin, when she had fully awakened.

"Mrs. Weatherspoon and Jo and even the kittens! They're all gone. And their suitcases are gone!"

"What? Not possible," said Marlin. "Where could they all have gotten to?"

Then Natasha and Charlie were up and came running into Fiona's and Marlin's bedroom to jump about on their cold, excited little feet.

The girls were all in a state of wonder as they went downstairs and looked first at the snowy outside and then the downstairs with no signs of Jo or Mrs. Weatherspoon ever having been there. Even Jo's lentil supply had been taken.

"We *paid at least partly* for those lentils!" said Marlin in outrage.

"Never mind, who cares? Look, all the barley, all the nuts, everything Jo eats has been taken. But why would they leave and not tell us?" asked Fiona, who was rooting through the cupboards.

"And look, there are more presents!" said Charlie in excitement, just now discovering Mrs. Weatherspoon's gifts under the tree.

"Should we wait for them to get back before we open stockings?" asked Natasha.

"I don't think they're coming back," said Fiona.

"Let's ask Al if he knows where they've gone," said Marlin, just as they saw him tromping through the snow from his trailer.

"Well!" he said when he came blustering in, stomping

snow off his boots. "A white Christmas! This is one for the books! And pretty lucky it didn't snow twelve hours ago or it would have sunk my big Christmas surprise."

"You got rid of Jo and Mrs. Weatherspoon!" said Fiona.

"No!" said Marlin. "Did you actually do it? How? You're no smarter than us!"

"Marlin..." said Fiona.

"Well, he's not."

"Well, I guess I am, smarty-pants," said Al. "Although it was actually your solution, Marlin."

"Did you take them into Shoreline and get them a hotel room for Christmas or something?" asked Marlin.

"No, how would that have been your solution, you never suggested that and I never do things by halves, you should know that by now. I gave them a little surprise Christmas present of their own yesterday. Train tickets across Canada. One-way, of course, and at the end of their train trip, airline tickets home. One-way too. My treat. It was your idea, Marlin. I just paid for it and it's the best investment I ever made. Mrs. Weatherspoon didn't want to take them, but I assured her it was to thank her properly for the year of her life she gave up to take care of you girls. She wanted to say good-bye to you before she left but I told her the only seats left on the train were for Christmas Day and I grabbed them and that they had to be on the ferry on Christmas Eve or they wouldn't make the train. And I said they mustn't say a thing beforehand because you girls would be so bereft at their leaving that such a devastating tearful good-bye would just about ruin Christmas for you."

"And they believed you?" scoffed Marlin.

"Oh, they believed me. Especially Jo, who with a free trip ahead couldn't wait to get started. She didn't think to question why *she* was getting a free trip too; she was too busy taking advantage of it."

"Naturally," agreed Marlin.

"So—merry Christmas!" said Al. "And a happy new year."

Marlin was so grateful and excited at this news that she dashed over and hugged Al, which seemed to surprise him no end. None of the girls had ever hugged him before.

"Is it okay, Fiona?" he asked her, and he looked so worried that she relented. She suddenly saw her reluctance to take help from him not as a matter of pride but as a refusal of something and she realized he had wanted into their family, and that was what she had been pushing away. Feeling that he would displace her parents. But now she knew it wasn't like that. He could never displace them, he was his own addition, separate from who her parents had been, a different kind of member of the family altogether, who in joining them took nothing away from who her family had been before her parents' death. "It's fine," she said. "I mean, it's more than fine. Thank you."

He nodded.

"Well, all right, all right," said Al. "Let's not overreact. I wanted them gone as much as you. What's for Christmas breakfast?"

Then Marlin put the Christmas casserole in to cook and they all settled in the living room to open their stockings and the meager supply of presents under the tree.

"Jo and Mrs. Weatherspoon found their presents, I guess," said Fiona as she sorted through them.

"Jo took them," said Al. "I saw her scoop them up and put them in a shopping bag."

"I'm surprised she didn't take ours as well," said Marlin.

"Marlin, she's *gone*," said Fiona.

"Right!" said Marlin, and for once let things drop.

Then everyone opened their toques and declared them just the thing for this snowy weather. Marlin's packages were jars full of old-fashioned pulled taffy in many colors that she and Jeannie had made at Jeannie's house.

Charlie popped some into her mouth immediately.

"*Two* presents this year!" she said. "I like this new tradition."

"Three," said Marlin. "Everyone gets three if you count Al's present of sending away Mrs. Weatherspoon and Jo."

"Four," said Al. "You don't think that's all you're getting, do you? What kind of guardian would I be if that were all I gave you?"

"The best, trust me," said Marlin, who was luxuriating in eating pulled taffy for breakfast without anyone commenting on it.

"Nevertheless," said Al, "I have something special for each of you. Actually, everyone gets to share a bit in everyone else's present so I don't know how many that makes for everyone—"

"Wait a second," interrupted Fiona. "I just noticed. The kittens and the litter box. They're gone too. Is that our fourth present? Did Mrs. Weatherspoon take them on the train with her?"

"No, on both counts. That's not your fourth present and Mrs. Weatherspoon didn't take them. No, the cats went to Mr. Pennypacker."

"Mr. Pennypacker!" exclaimed Marlin.

Mr. Pennypacker was the cantankerous family lawyer whom Al had dubbed a garden gnome. Fiona rarely dealt with him anymore because Al had taken over most of the girls' business affairs so he, instead, saw him on a regular basis.

"Yeah, when I talked to him last week he was saying how hard it was to get pets from the SPCA. That he wanted a cat but they never seemed to have any. They only had puppies."

"Puppies!" said Natasha. "Jo said they didn't have any puppies."

"Jo said a lot of things," said Marlin.

"Anyhow, I said I had a couple of kittens and if he would take *both* of them he could have them as our Christmas present to him. They even came with food, food dishes, litter box, litter, toys, the whole shebang. He was delighted. He is renaming them Stalin and Mussolini."

"What kind of names are those?" said Marlin. "Naming them after tyrants."

"He decided to name them that after I told him, in the spirit of fair disclosure, the kind of destruction they had wrought on the house ever since arriving. It turns out the garden gnome has a sense of humor. Anyhow, he was delighted," said Al. "I dropped them off last night when I was taking the ladies to the ferry. And now if we can get on with things I'd like to give you each your present."

"Ooooo, more presents!" cried Charlie, bouncing on the couch.

"First of all, Natasha." Al handed her an envelope. Out of it she took a photo.

"What is this?" she asked, studying the picture.

"What does it look like?" asked Al. "Don't tell me you don't recognize your ledge?"

Natasha studied the photo more closely and then cried out in delight. She passed the photo around. At first the girls just saw the ledge and then they saw wooden steps going up a tree and high in the branches a wonderful tree house complete with a roof and porch and windows.

"You built Natasha her house in the trees!" said Marlin.

"Yes, and I had a time doing it. I am not, by nature, a carpenter," said Al proudly. "But I studied the plans and worked it out. It took me most of November while you were all in school."

"She can be up with the birds of prey when they gather," said Fiona.

"Exactly. And that's why I didn't want you going up the mountain, Nat. I wasn't worried about a mudslide as I said but I had to think of something to keep you from going up and discovering it before Christmas."

"Thank you," said Natasha, getting up and heading for the door.

"Nat," said Fiona, laughing. "At least wait until everyone has gotten their presents."

"Oh," said Nat, and sat back down.

"I take that as a triumph," said Al. "She likes her present. Well done, me. Now, Fiona, you're next."

He handed her a box.

Fiona opened it wondering what in the world he had gotten her but when she had the wrapping off she could hardly believe it and sat staring mutely at it.

"So?" said Al.

"I can't believe you got me a cell phone," said Fiona. "After everything you've said about them."

"Well, when you went missing and after I found you by

the side of the road, I realized I was wrong. If you'd had a cell you could have phoned. I may be a dinosaur but even a dinosaur can learn new tricks. Now, when I talked about everyone sharing the presents, I am assuming everyone, at Nat's invitation, of course, can visit the tree house and equally, if any of you girls plans to be going to town with a friend or something similar, I expect you to take the cell phone."

"You know you have to have a plan for that," said Marlin, unable to stop herself. "And if we use it here, we need data."

"Marlin!" said Fiona.

"That's okay, Fiona," said Al. "As it happens, Marlin, I did get a plan and data. So maybe not such a dinosaur as you think. Now, Charlie, I have to go to the trailer to get your present."

Al rose to his feet and left the house to return a few minutes later with a big box just as the girls were hunched over the cell phone, playing with it. But they put it down at the same time Al put down the box he was carrying. The box seemed to have a life of its own, moving from side to side and almost tipping over of its own accord. Then Al said to Charlie, "This is for you. Go ahead and open it."

Charlie ran over, opened it, and shrieked.

"Good-bye kittens, hello puppies!" said Al as all the girls rushed to kneel around the box and Charlie picked up the squirmier of the pair and held it to her chest.

"You're going to have to house-train them and generally care for them," warned Al. "That's part of the deal."

"Oh, they're so beautiful," said Charlie.

"Stick and Feather," said Al.

"No," said Charlie seriously, picking up the other. "They don't look like Stick and Feather, they're too wiggly."

"They're adorable," said Marlin, taking one from Charlie and cuddling it. The small brown puppies were a mass of energy and soon they were being passed from girl to girl with everyone ooing and aahing contentedly.

"They're perfect. Whatever breed they are, they're perfect," said Natasha.

"What breed *are* they?" asked Marlin.

"They're no breed, they're mutts," said Al. "And they're Charlie's present because I think she wanted them the most and asked for them the longest but they're, like all the presents, for everyone to share one way or another. And I hope you're not too disappointed that they aren't purebred."

"Jeannie says you don't want a purebred anyway," said Marlin. "She has a mutt. She says purebreds get overbred and have all kinds of problems."

"Yes," said Charlie. "You don't want a purebred. Jeannie is right. I love them. I love this one especially."

She picked up the one with a white mask.

"Charlie, you're not supposed to love one best," said Fiona.

"But I do," said Charlie.

"Maybe," suggested Marlin with a glint, remembering what Fiona had told her Charlie had said, "she loves that one best downstairs and the other best upstairs."

The others didn't get the reference but Fiona laughed.

"Let's name them," said Charlie.

"Before we get to that," said Marlin, who'd been thinking, "I'd like to know how you managed to blow all that money on tickets for Mrs. Weatherspoon and Jo. Those must have cost a packet. Is that why you were frantically doing those magazine pieces? Is that why you were too busy to take Fiona into Shoreline?"

"I wasn't *unusually* too busy, Marlin. Jeez, you act as if, if I hadn't been so motivated I would have been just sitting around watching clouds pass by. I was *working* as *usual.* You guys act like I have nothing to do but chauffeur you around!" Al began a well-known rant and Fiona glared at Marlin, who rolled her eyes. "Like I can drop everything anytime you whistle. I was doing the magazine pieces *after* I'd already had a windfall, as a matter of fact, because a few weeks ago I got my book accepted and a big fat advance. I could have done the tickets and Christmas *anyway* because I'm not the pauper you seem to think but I decided to splurge on those tickets for all of our sakes. And I didn't mention my book sale because frankly, I thought it would depress Marlin."

Marlin looked thunderstruck and then, just as Al feared, deeply upset but she pulled herself together enough to say, "Congratulations. Well, I said you would get your novel snatched up immediately, didn't I?"

"Aren't you going to ask me why I feel comfortable telling you about it now?" asked Al.

"Because you are explaining where the money for the tickets came from," said Marlin. "Because I was stupid enough to ask."

"Think again," said Al.

"Because that was *your* Christmas present," said Marlin. "You got your book published. That's great. Best Christmas present ever, I'm sure."

"Gee, Marlin," said Al, his eyes twinkling. "For a girl smart enough to be an author, you're a little slow putting together the pieces here."

Marlin stared at him in barely concealed irritation. It was bad enough his book was published, but now he was calling her slow?

"I couldn't tell you about my book being published before because it would upset you. But I can now..." hinted Al.

"Because..." said Fiona, suddenly understanding and leaping to her feet in excitement.

"Let Marlin get it herself," said Al, putting a restraining hand on Fiona's forearm.

"Because..." whispered Marlin slowly as light dawned. "Because my book is being published?"

"Merry Christmas!" said Al.

"And happy new year!" crowed Fiona.

"I got a letter from Steve four days ago. He wanted to call you, Marl, but I wouldn't let him because I wanted to save it for today. Because I couldn't think of a present that would make you happier."

The sounds Marlin made would long be remembered by her sisters. When she settled down Al gave her more details but she hardly heard him. A greater happiness could not have come to her.

"Are you mad at me for waiting four days to tell you?" asked Al when she had calmed down enough to sit still.

"No, because Jo was still here four days ago and she would have found some way to kill all the joy," said Marlin.

But everyone doubted that even Jo could have killed Marlin's joy, so great was it.

When all the congratulations and shrieking were over Charlie said with her unerring logic, "But that present didn't come from you, it came from Steve. Or from that publisher."

"Or from herself, really. *She* did it," said Al. "You're quite right, Charlie. My gift to Marlin pales so much by comparison that I almost didn't want to bother giving it to her, but I will. Like all your gifts it's one you can all enjoy. I got you the Food Network, Marlin, so you can keep up with the competition and see what kinds of things are happening in your field."

There was great happiness for hours after that.

Al went back to his trailer for a while and Marlin got busy making the turkey dinner with a whole turkey instead of parts this time.

Natasha ran up to check out the tree house. The others said they would all take a walk up there later in the day. When Natasha came back to the house to play with the puppies her cheeks were glowing from the cold and her delight in such a perfect retreat in the woods all her own.

It wasn't until nearly evening that Charlie pointed out they hadn't opened what they were sure were their religious tracts or Bible stories from Mrs. Weatherspoon. When they did, they found to their surprise that the books Mrs. Weatherspoon had gotten each of them were not religious tracts. She got Natasha and Charlie each two of the Mrs. Piggle-Wiggle books so that they owned the whole set. She got Fiona *Islandia* and Marlin *Eight Cousins*. She wrote *My favorite book at your age* on each of the flyleaves.

"How kind, how generous of her," said Fiona. "It's more like the Mrs. Weatherspoon I remember."

"Maybe she will rub off on Jo someday rather than vice versa," said Marlin, who was so happy she was willing to be optimistic about even this.

"Hey," said Charlie. "I know what to name the puppies. This one can be Piggle. And this one, because he won't stop moving, can be Wiggle."

And everyone agreed those were the perfect names. At least for Christmas Day.

Then Al came back inside and they all took a long walk through the snow to admire the tree house.

Then everyone's toes began to freeze, for they only had rubber boots that didn't keep them warm long in the snow, so they raced back to the house, where all the girls helped put Marlin's classic turkey dinner on the table. After, they all stood behind the table as Al took a photo of the sisters behind the turkey with Natasha and Charlie holding up the puppies. Then Fiona took the cell phone and insisted Al get behind the table with the others and she took a photo. Then *everyone* insisted on taking a photo until finally Marlin cried, "ENOUGH! LET'S EAT!"

The phone rang during dinner, which for a moment stopped everyone's hearts.

"It's Mrs. Weatherspoon and Jo saying their train was canceled," said Marlin in dread.

But Fiona answered it and it was only Carol Simmons of the new church saying they were sorry the girls hadn't made the noon service as Jo had said they would.

"I may have promised Mrs. Weatherspoon on the way to the ferry that I would bring you and forgot," said

Al as they listened to Fiona talk to Carol Simmons on speakerphone.

"And promised Jo too, I guess," said Marlin. "She was so adamant we go today."

"No, I think Jo lost interest in you the second she left the house," said Al.

"Well, thank you," they all heard Fiona say to Carol Simmons. "But we won't be joining. I'm sorry they said we would but we won't and we wish you all the luck in the world with it." And then without further ado she hung up.

"Now *that's* the way to do it," said Al as Fiona returned to the table. "So what's for dessert?"

"I made a yule log," said Marlin, proudly carrying it to the table.

When Marlin put it down, Fiona stood up and squeaked, "Oh my God, *your* present, Al! From all of us. With all the excitement of Marlin's book being published, we totally forgot."

And she ran for the freezer and brought in his Dairy Queen cake. She put it on the table in front of Al and he just stared at it. When he said nothing and continued to stare, Marlin said, "It's a Dairy Queen cake."

"It's got all our names on it," said Natasha.

"Is it not the type you like?" asked Charlie.

"Like it, um, well, yeah, I like it," said Al, and he

appeared as if he didn't know where to look. "As a matter of fact, I like no kind better."

"I think you should eat it all yourself," said Marlin.

"He'll get fat," said Charlie, who clearly wanted some.

Al's only reply was to cut some for each of them and put it on the dessert plates next to the yule log slices Marlin was busy placing there.

Then they all piled onto the giant couch and put on one of the many recorded *Jeopardy!* shows.

Fiona thought about how interesting it was that you could share your life with some people and not at all with others.

Marlin was thinking that for months she had been concentrating so hard on the people she couldn't stand and how to deal with them that she had forgotten how lucky she was to be with these other people.

For the rest of the evening everyone ate too much cake with too much Dairy Queen ice cream and watched *Jeopardy!* until they were all almost too tired to move. Then Al returned to his trailer and everyone else went to bed.

Fiona lay on her back, her hands clasped behind her head, and stared out at the stars. It was a crisp cold clear winter's night. Turning to Marlin, she was surprised to find tears running slowly down her face.

"Hey," said Fiona. "What is it? You've been bursting all day. Your *book* is being published."

"Did you feel today," said Marlin, floundering around for a way to express it, "despite everything, in some part of you sad?"

"I think," said Fiona slowly, "that there is a part of me that will always be sad every Christmas, every birthday. I think we carry certain sadnesses with us our whole lives. Even when we don't consciously feel or think about them, they are there."

"Do you think that will ever go away?" asked Marlin.

"No," said Fiona.

They were quiet a moment.

"But," said Fiona, thinking of these times which like all times would not last forever, lying in a cot next to Marlin's, discussing the whole world and their own rocky passage through it. Watching the big dipper, eternal but her own so long as she was there to see it. She would not always be with these people she loved but she would always carry them in her heart. "I think we carry certain happinesses with us too. That they are always there with us. That they never go away. Our whole lives."

They lay looking out the window.

The stars burned through the heavens and the icy layers of the sky.

"Merry Christmas," said Fiona.

"Merry Christmas," said Marlin.

ACKNOWLEDGMENTS

Thank you as always to the following people:
Andrea Cascardi
Margaret Ferguson
Lynne Missen
Ken Setterington